"Not just anybody can make sudden death, funerals, too much gin, eye injuries, forbidden lust, days of reckoning, and the car trip from all-kinds-of-insane into something hilarious, moving, fresh, and hip. But Daniel Ehrenhaft can and does with *The After Life*. I don't know how he does it—he's some kind of weird rock star/writer/alien hybrid—but I don't care. I just want him to keep writing so I can keep reading."

—*New York Times* best-selling author Libba Bray

praise for
DANIEL EHRENHAFT'S
previous books

"A sweet, hilariously told, sad-but-true tale of high school angst."
—Cecily von Ziegesar, *New York Times* best-selling author of *Gossip Girl*, on *Tell it to Naomi*

★ "A fresh, effervescent combination of mystery, adventure, and teen angst." —*Booklist*, starred review for *Drawing a Blank: or How I Tried to Solve a Mystery, End a Feud, and Land the Girl of My Dreams*

"A smartly written, thoroughly engrossing tale."
—*Publisher's Weekly*, review for *The Last Dog on Earth*

"Teens will enjoy the lighthearted romance and its unlikely hero."
—*Booklist*, review for *10 Things to Do Before I Die*

the after life

a novel by
DANIEL EHRENHAFT

razor bill

The After Life

RAZORBILL

Published by the Penguin Group
Penguin Young Readers Group
345 Hudson Street, New York, New York 10014, U.S.A.
Penguin Group (USA) Inc., 375 Hudson Street, New York, New York 10014, U.S.A.
Penguin Group (Canada), 90 Eglinton Avenue East, Suite 700, Toronto, Ontario,
Canada M4P 2Y3 (a division of Pearson Penguin Canada Inc.)
Penguin Books Ltd, 80 Strand, London WC2R 0RL, England
Penguin Ireland, 25 St Stephen's Green, Dublin 2, Ireland (a division of Penguin
Books Ltd)
Penguin Group (Australia), 250 Camberwell Road, Camberwell, Victoria 3124,
Australia (a division of Pearson Australia Group Pty Ltd)
Penguin Books India Pvt Ltd, 11 Community Centre, Panchsheel Park, New Delhi –
110 017, India
Penguin Group (NZ), Cnr Airborne and Rosedale Roads, Albany, Auckland 1310,
New Zealand (a division of Pearson New Zealand Ltd)
Penguin Books (South Africa) (Pty) Ltd, 24 Sturdee Avenue, Rosebank, Johannesburg
2196, South Africa

Penguin Books Ltd, Registered Offices: 80 Strand, London WC2R 0RL, England

10 9 8 7 6 5 4 3 2 1

Library of Congress Cataloging-in-Publication Data

Ehrenhaft, Daniel.
  The after life : a novel / by Daniel Ehrenhaft.
    p. cm.
  Summary: When Will Shephard's estranged millionaire father dies, a bizarre
clause in the will sends him on a drug- and alcohol-fueled road trip from
Miami to New York with his twin half-siblings.
  ISBN 1-59514-080-8
  [1. Alcoholism--Fiction. 2. Drug abuse--Fiction. 3. Brothers and
sisters--Fiction. 4. Twins--Fiction. 5. Fathers--Fiction. 6. Automobile
travel--Fiction.] I. Title.
  PZ7.E3235Af 2006
  [Fic]--dc22
                                        2006013285

Printed in the United States of America

For Liesa Abrams, the wizard behind the curtain.

We are what we pretend to be,
so we must be careful about what we pretend to be.
—Kurt Vonnegut

prologue:

THE APPLICATION ESSAY[1]

[1] In two drafts

Will Shepherd's Application Essay for the Wiltshire School, First Draft

In 750 words or less, please describe a major turning point in your life.

"Nobody likes a quitter, Will."

That was the last thing my uncle Pete said to me, right before he crashed an E-Z-Lern driver's ed car into a gas pump. You may have heard about the explosion in the news last fall—it was in Brooklyn. It was very noisy and violent. At first everybody assumed terrorists were responsible. The cops and the government and whoever else sealed off the block for several days to clean up the debris and investigate.

The idea that anybody would suspect my uncle Pete of terrorism is actually sort of funny. The authorities even laughed about it later. When you think of terrorists, you generally think of lean and intense young fanatics, men with haunted black eyes. Pete was loud and chubby, and he was a booze hound, and his eyes were always bloodshot, like two red jelly beans. He'd finally decided to get his driver's license at the age of forty-nine. Why, I don't know. He worked at home as a "freelance journalist" (whatever that means), so he never really had to drive anywhere. Besides, he'd always reveled in being a nondriver. "Being a designated passenger gives me more time to drink," he liked to joke. When he told me he was enrolling in driver's ed, I thought he was pulling my leg. To be honest, I thought he was looking to disappear for a few hours a week to try out a new bar. I decided to tag along with him on his first official lesson, just to make sure.

The joke was on me. For once, Pete was telling the truth.

That fateful afternoon, he said he needed a smoke before he got behind the wheel, to calm his nerves. I wasn't surprised. Pete smoked over a pack of unfiltered Lucky Strikes a day. Smoking is forbidden in E-Z-Lern cars, but that didn't stop Pete from lighting up in the parking lot. Unfortunately, his instructor, Dexter—a guy barely half his age—got annoyed. Pete just laughed and told him to "mellow out." He said that he would be done in a minute. I mumbled that maybe Pete shouldn't make trouble; maybe he should just quit smoking, period. He wasn't exactly healthy. His flesh was heavily lined and gray, like a veal cutlet. Besides, he was turning over a new leaf with this learning-to-drive thing. He was growing up.

I said, "Pete, if you don't stop smoking, you'll probably drop dead before you ever even get a chance to drive on your own. You really should quit, you know?"

Pete exhaled a deep cloud of smoke. He glanced at Dexter, then at me, and then smirked and rattled off those five words:

"Nobody likes a quitter, Will."

Dexter burst out laughing. Pete winked at me and stubbed out the cigarette. They both climbed into the car. I told them I'd wait in the parking lot. Pete waved good-bye, and without warning he gunned the engine, plowing straight into the gas station across the street. To this day, I can still see the first flash of fire and smell that weird smell: like a mixture of burnt plastic and lit matches and new asphalt on a hot, sunny day. I try not to think about it.

Which I guess is the point of this essay: at first I was really good at not thinking about Pete. For a while, in fact (except for the funeral), I managed to avoid thinking about him altogether, except for just one other time: the night I tried to have sex with Shelly Plotnick.

This was about three weeks later, one of the first times I'd left the apartment since the whole thing happened. At my mom's insistence, I went to a gallery opening for one of her clients. She's an agent for painters and sculptors.

I used to go to gallery openings all the time.

The fall season is when the New York art scene really comes alive—everyone is looking to make money. There are openings every night of the week. This is no exaggeration. If you're a clever bottom-feeder, you can live on free wine and cheese for months so long as you don't mind standing around and you own a nice jacket. And when you're the only child of a single mother—a mother who happens to represent some of "the most provocative up-and-coming Picassos" (her words)—then you don't even have to be that clever.

This particular opening was at a hole-in-the-wall gallery in Tribeca. It was called "Haiku Sexy." The artist was a Latino, a guy named Jesus. (Pronounced hey-SOOS. Also, one name only, like Madonna.) He wrote offensive haikus in calligraphy and illustrated them with nutty cartoons. Here's an example:

I read somewhere once
Midgets have the nicest butts
Because they're so small!

I can't draw, but you can probably imagine what the accompanying cartoon looked like.

Anyway, as soon as I arrived with Mom, I headed straight for the little bar area. There I met Shelly Plotnick. She was a brunette, a few years older than me—a tad scrawny, but cute. She wore a black V-neck sweater, low-cut. I love black sweaters. The circumstances of our meeting: both of us reached for the last plastic cup of free chardonnay. I let her have it. She blushed and introduced herself. She told me she was a junior at NYU. She was alone. Her friends had apparently left in a huff, offended by Jesus and his art.

Luckily, the bartender broke out some more plastic cups and poured more chardonnay.

Shelly and I proceeded to get plastered. I didn't do much talking. It didn't matter. Shelly liked the sound of her own voice. She spoke at length about her dorm on John Street. It was brand new, and there were kitchens, and she had a private room in a suite. She allowed me to stare at her meager cleavage. She told me that she loved going out on Monday nights because Monday was the new Thursday. Eventually she asked me what I was doing at the party. I explained that my mom was Jesus's agent and a friend of the gallery owner and that I'd been going to parties like this since I'd been old enough to walk. Like many other girls I'd tried to hook up with over the years, Shelly thought that this was "SO COOL."

When the gallery opening ended, Shelly invited me back to John Street. I looked over at Mom and waved good-bye. She gave me a thumbs-up. She was drunk too.

Shelly's dorm was, true to her description, very nice. It was brand new, and there was a kitchen, and she had a private room in her suite.

After a few beers, Shelly shoved her tongue into my

mouth. Soon we were naked. I felt pretty decent, definitely better than I'd felt in a while. Plus, I was living out a lifelong fantasy: I was having sex with a college girl before I was actually *in* college. But for some unfathomable reason, I couldn't perform. It was horrifying. Shelly Plotnick was right there, moaning and panting, and that certain crucial part of my anatomy refused to cooperate. There was nothing I could do. There was nothing she could do, either. And the worst part was that I suddenly started thinking about Uncle Pete, smiling at me next to that E-Z-Lern car and puffing on that Lucky Strike.

"Nobody likes a quitter, Will."

Will Shepherd's Application Essay for the Wiltshire School, Final Draft

In 750 words or less, please describe a major turning point in your life.

What is this, anyway—psychotherapy or an application form? Just kidding. Fine, I will try to describe such a turning point, but just so you know: I am going to tell you the most INCREDIBLE STORY, which revolves around what happened to me before and after I watched my uncle Pete crash a car and burn to death right in front of my eyes.

If you want to talk major turning points, you got yourself a humdinger.

And by the way, not to pat myself on the back, but isn't my opening paragraph shocking and witty? Isn't it brutally honest? I think it demonstrates both originality[2] and self-awareness.[3] On the basis of that alone, you should let me into your school. That and my astonishing

---

[2] Originality: the courage to break the standard application essay formula by opening with such a controversial pronouncement—and a sarcastic rhetorical question, no less.

[3] Self-awareness: realizing that by writing about such a tragedy, I am doing something that every other jackass who is applying to Wiltshire is also probably doing in one form or another.

vocabulary. And the fact that my half sister, Liz, goes to Wiltshire. In these patriotic and religiously fundamentalist times, family (even half family) counts for a lot, right? Plus, there are my devastating good looks. I didn't enclose a photo, but please take my word for it.

So I'm sure you already know a little something about my recent history: that I went to S—— until the beginning of my senior year and that they kicked me out for failing to show up at school for one full month. And you probably also know that after my expulsion, I underwent major analysis and was encouraged by a well-meaning shrink named Dr. Brown (a really nice guy) to get over my anger at Pete for accidentally killing himself, and to ingest a variety of "meds," and blah, blah, blah (hey, how many people write *blah, blah, blah* on an application essay? Huh? That's bold too), and here I am, at age nineteen, floundering. I am about to move from Tribeca to the Upper East Side with Mom, Pete's younger sister, who is a failing artists' agent. And I am trying to get into Wiltshire for a belated senior year so I can finally graduate, then go to college, then stake out my piece of the American Dream—which is . . . well, it used to be forty acres and a mule, but now I think it's something called "Homeland Security."

Many run-on sentences, I know. Forgive me. Back to the most INCREDIBLE STORY:

It is a story about a boy named Will Shepherd. I am going to tell it in the third person because it will allow me to be detached and objective. It is all one major turning point (or a series of related major turning points), but I have to tell you, it will run longer than 750 words. I will try to be succinct. Remember, though, this is Will Shepherd's life we're talking about. So have a heart, and be patient if you can. The payoff will be huge.

Part One: The Plan

Will Shepherd was a great guy. He woke up on the first day of school last year knowing that it wasn't just *any* first day. It was the start of a triumphant new era. And as he stood before the bathroom mirror, staring at his naked body—ignoring his hangover and smiling confidently—he saw his entire existence as a giant rehearsal leading up to this moment.

NO MORE DISAPPOINTMENTS.

He was shedding the identity of a skinny, smart-mouthed, semi-alcoholic clown. It was senior year: time to kick things into high gear. He would get straight A's. He would ace the SATs. He would stop attending his mom's art parties and gallery openings, where he always got drunk. He would also stop hanging out so much with his uncle Pete, who was a heavy drinker in his own right. Instead, Will would join school clubs (the debate team, maybe?) and perform community service. And then he would get into Yale. And then he would finally call Dad.[4] That would be the REAL triumph. "Oh, hey, Dad, how've you been? How are my half siblings, the twins? The ones

---

[4] Dad: Forrest Shepherd II, enormous shitbag and sole inheritor of a medical plastics fortune worth roughly $60,000,000 (or more)—money Will won't ever see because Dad inexplicably abandoned Will and his mom when Will was nine months old, then moved in with a new wife and had the twins.

I've never met in person, even though they live just a subway ride away? Liz and Kyle? Anyway, I just wanted to tell you: I'm still following in Uncle Pete's footsteps. Uncle Pete never learned to drive, and neither will I. But I did get into Yale on a full National Merit Scholarship or some such, so the fact is, I'll never *have* to learn how to drive, because, as Uncle Pete says, 'driving is a waste of gas.' Besides, when I graduate, I will instantly become rich and famous, and a chauffeured limo will take me everywhere I want to go—so when we talk once a year on my birthday like always, you can drop the shit you said last time about how I'm a 'slacker like Pete,' because at least I EARNED my money, unlike you. And if there's ever been a case of the pot calling the kettle black, it's you calling Pete a slacker. He has a job, at least."

And then Will would hang up. That was the plan, anyway.

Part Two: The Expulsion

The plan didn't quite work out. First, Uncle Pete changed his mind and decided that he *did* want to learn to drive. Shortly thereafter, he incinerated himself in the aforementioned crash.

After that, Will had difficulty focusing on his long-term goals. He took a few days off from school and stayed at home just to regroup. He passed the time the way most people in mourning do—by abandoning any productive activities, self-medicating, and watching *Law & Order* reruns. The one time he did leave his house (to attend a gallery opening for one of his mom's clients), he wound up involved in a disastrous tryst with a college girl.[5] And then a strange thing began to happen. He found himself *unable* to leave home. He refused to go back to S——. Maybe it was the thought of seeing his friends in person and having to explain what happened to Uncle Pete. Maybe it was the thought of having to talk about how he felt. Maybe it was the thought of seeing some kid get into an E-Z-Lern driver's ed car outside school. Whatever the reason, Mom freaked out and sent Will to Dr. Brown, a very nice man who specializes in troubled adolescents and agoraphobics and who plied him with "meds" and blah, blah, blah.[6] But Will still couldn't bring himself to go back to school.

Finally S—— got fed up. They sent him a letter asking him to withdraw.

Luckily, Will was home to receive the letter, so he saw it before Mom did.

Part Three: The Confession

That night, Will drank five beers to prepare himself to tell Mom the bad news. He dreaded conversations like this. Real moments of crisis always forced him to confront an ugly reality, which was that Mom suffered from depression. There was no doubt about it. He probably hadn't seen her laugh—really, truly crack up—in years. Even worse, whenever he tried to bring up the possibility that

[5] The details are far too sordid to discuss in an application essay.

[6] Blah, blah, blah: in this case, a defense mechanism used to avoid going into the specifics of my therapy, which I don't feel like sharing with strangers, no offense.

she might be depressed, she denied it. Like at Uncle Pete's funeral. Perfect example. When they got home, she described herself as "still, at root, a very happy person." She'd said this apropos of nothing. As far as Will knew, notwithstanding the premature death of a sibling, "very happy people" didn't cry so much, or have such a faraway look in their eyes, or drink wine at three in the afternoon, or maintain fully stocked pharmacies in their medicine cabinets. Not that Will planned to bring any of this up. He planned to tell Mom that he'd been asked to withdraw from S——, and then he planned to take two Zolofts and wash them down with the plastic bottle of Smirnoff hidden under his bed.

Oddly, Mom didn't seem all that disappointed when he told her. She didn't even seem sad. She almost seemed to be expecting it: she informed him that he'd been asked to withdraw from S—— because he never dressed appropriately for class.

"I don't know," Will said. "I think it was more because I stopped showing up."

"Well, maybe that's what they want you to think, dear," she said. "But the fact of the matter is that you dress like a little kid. You never even wore a jacket."

Will pointed out that jackets weren't required except for special occasions; moreover, dress codes in general were regressing as society advanced, and these days it was impossible to tell an eighteen-year-old from a forty-year-old—at least in terms of wardrobe and possibly much more. Respected teachers exposed their midriffs and wore the same nose pierces and baggy pants as their students. Compared to most of his classmates, in fact, Will dressed conservatively.

"You mean your former classmates, honey," she said. "Although I appreciate the trenchant commentary on the informal state of our declining culture. You know . . ." She didn't finish.

"What?" Will said.

"Nothing," she said. "What you said just reminded me of Forrest—and not necessarily in a bad way. That's all."

Will didn't answer. Was there a good way he could remind her of Dad? Forrest Shepherd II was the reason she was so weird and depressed in the first place. HE was the enormous shitbag who screwed them over. HE ran out on them, but HE still managed to keep almost all of the money because HE had the money to pay for a good lawyer To top it all off, HE was the EMBODIMENT of "the informal state of our declining culture." Yes, even more so than Uncle Pete. But Will decided not to get upset. If she wasn't going to let this latest catastrophe put her in a bad mood, then neither would he.

Part Four: The Months That Followed

In the months that followed, Will secretly stopped taking his "meds." They made him feel weird. He also stopped returning his friends' phone calls. Soon he didn't have any friends. Occasionally, when Mom had the energy, she nagged him about being a dropout. He dealt with it by obsessively cleaning the apartment for several hours each day.

"See?" he said. "I'm saving us the money on a maid."

He also thought of getting a learner's permit as a tribute to Pete but rejected the idea after his short annual birthday conversation with Dad, in which Dad said again that Will's inability to drive was "a bad symptom of some heavy issues." Will could have mentioned that he'd be better able to deal with these issues if Dad just sent him some of the money he was entitled to, AS HIS ABANDONED SON. Then again, he also could have mentioned that he was going through sort of a rough patch, seeing as he'd recently watched his uncle burn to a crisp—a subject Dad mysteriously chose to avoid. But why ruin an otherwise pleasant chat?

At one point, thoughts of suicide flitted through Will's brain. But he was never able to muster the courage to swallow a bottle of pills or take a header off the George Washington Bridge. Besides, he didn't have the money to pay for cab fare uptown.

Part Five: The Bombshell

One afternoon in May, Mom poured herself a large glass of wine and summoned Will to the kitchen. She tried to smile. The thing was . . . well, see, she wasn't doing quite as well financially as she'd previously suspected. The downtown art scene was drying up. Plus, she'd inherited Pete's credit card debt, which was somewhere in the high five figures.

Also, earlier in the day, she'd talked with her accountant, a guy named Joe. In the eighties, acting on Joe's advice, she'd invested the majority of her modest divorce settlement in the stock market. Now various corporate accounting scandals had rendered 78 percent of the stock worthless. She was far from destitute, obviously, but she was going to have to make some changes—the first of which was to sell the apartment. Which was a good thing. Because in the end, she wanted to get out of the neighborhood. What with the closing galleries, the confusing new recycling laws, the traffic . . . it was time to leave. Joe's news was basically just the kick in the behind she needed to get going. She planned to move to a small rental apartment uptown as soon as possible. Things were happening uptown. A new art scene was thriving up there.

Dad was uptown too. But that really didn't matter. Uptown was a big place.

To make a long story short: Mom made arrangements with the Wiltshire School for Will to send in an application. Apparently, Wiltshire was a GREAT school, just like S——. Plus they had a dress code, a real dress code. You had to wear a jacket and tie every day. The only caveat: Will's private education would end there. His psychotherapy alone was like another tuition, and there was no way Mom would stop sending Will to Dr. Brown. No way! So she wouldn't be able to afford four years of college. Not unless one of her artists suddenly took off. In other words, Will would have to do well enough at Wiltshire to earn a full scholarship—ironically, just as he had dreamed of doing when Pete was alive and he still fantasized about getting the best of Dad . . . that is, if Wiltshire accepted him at all. If not, he would have to go to public school.

On the plus side, they had a family connection at Wiltshire (remember?), which might help him. Will's half sister, Liz, was a student. Yes, the same Liz whom Dad had chosen over Will, whom Dad had raised uptown (less than four miles away from HIS ABANDONED SON) with his new wife—that being Cindy What's-her-face, a skanky Wiccan who dressed, true to her religion, like a witch. Or so he'd heard from Mom. He'd never actually seen Cindy What's-her-face, not even in pictures. In fact, the last time he'd seen Dad was ten years ago, when Dad had inexplicably mailed Will a photo of himself, Kyle, and Liz, posing with a whiskered transvestite. Apparently, the enormous shitbag had taken his beloved twins to see *Cats*.

Anyway, if Will got into Wiltshire, maybe he and Liz could forge the relationship they'd never had, as family. (Or half family, at least.)

"I'm sorry, honey," Mom concluded. She took a long sip of wine. "But sooner or later, we all have to learn to deal constructively with stress."

Will had to admit it: Mom was right. He'd never learned to deal constructively with stress. He'd never learned to deal with stress at all—period. Before Uncle Pete's accident, the only stress he'd ever felt was a sporadic anxiety about a possible drinking problem. And he'd always managed to forget about that after a few free plastic cups of chardonnay. His life had pretty much been one long, stress-free party. No, *party* is the wrong word. It had been a great big PROMISE of a party: a lifelong preview of a rock-star-like orgy lurking just around the bend, of the life Dad lived. And now, thanks to a dead uncle and corrupt CEOs and a wilting downtown art scene, that promise had been broken.

SO PLEASE LET WILL SHEPHERD INTO YOUR SCHOOL!!! GIVE HIM A CHANCE!!!

I told you the payoff was going to be huge, didn't I?

Love,
Will Shepherd

PS: Describing a "major turning point" seems like sort of a dumb assignment, doesn't it?
PPS: I was drunk when I wrote most of this. Just kidding.

part I:

THE FAMILY REUNION*

*With a couple of flashbacks

chapter 1

I was born thirty years too late.

Will Shepherd said this to himself a lot these days. It popped into his head whenever he saw a large crowd of kids his age. It had turned into a sort of mantra, a means of coping with the unfortunate fact that he was socially challenged. (The term *socially challenged* was preferable to the term *a basket case who lost all his friends last year because he freaked out after his uncle's death*.) But when he stepped through the doors of the Wiltshire School for the first time . . . *My God, look how young they are.*

The hall was packed with children. Some had braces. Many had zits. All wore the Wiltshire uniform: blue jumpers for the girls, blue blazers and ties for the boys. *What am I thinking?* he asked himself. There was nothing wrong with being a dropout. Being a dropout had a certain renegade respectability. Many great men were dropouts. Boys too. But at nearly twenty, Will was neither. He was too old to be a dropout *or* a high school student. He was merely pathetic: a freak, a comic anomaly—like Adam Sandler in that movie about that annoying guy who goes back to kindergarten . . . or Robin Williams in that movie about the annoying old man who has the body of a kid . . . or wait. Was he thinking about a movie with *both* of them? Had they even been in a movie together?

Hmm. His brain hurt. He shouldn't have snuck that final beer last night.

The doors slammed behind him. A couple of kids turned. They looked at him the way he might look at week-old salad.

"You can't let the door slam," one of them said.

"Whoops," Will said. "Sorry."

They went back to talking among themselves.

Will scoured the hall for any sign of his half sister. Not that he really wanted to see her. No, on top of everything else, he'd made a mistake. He shouldn't have given in to the urge to get in touch with Liz before school started. But last week, after four quick shots of vodka and several dozen repetitions of another secret mantra ("She's your FAMILY, asshole"), he'd found himself dialing Dad's house. And she'd answered.

Liz: Hello?

Will: Uh . . . yeah, hi. (*Coughing.*) Is, um, is Liz there, please?

Liz: Ned? Ned Parrish? Is that you?

Will: Uh . . . um, no. This is Will. You know . . . your, um, half brother.

Liz: Oh my God! Will! Are you SERIOUS?

Will: Yeah.

Liz: Oh my God. How ARE you? I heard about your uncle! I'm so sorry!

Will: Thanks.

Liz: But look, I am so PSYCHED, because Dad said that you're going to Wiltshire. Is that true?

Will: Uh . . . yeah.

Liz: Oh my God. Look, we have to get together. I mean, this is bullshit, right? I can't believe I've never even MET you. We're FAMILY. I don't care about any of Dad's crap. He's a lunatic. I want to see you in person. The problem is, we're going to Miami, and I don't get back until late Sunday night. . . . (*A pause.*) I'll tell you what. I'll e-mail you a photo of me, and then you'll know what I look like. I have comparative lit with Ms. Thompson first period, so—

Will: I'm in that class too.

Liz: You ARE? Oh my GOD! That is SO COOL!

And so on.

It seemed Will could do no wrong with his half sister—on the phone at least. He hadn't known what to expect, but he hadn't expected *that*. Actually, he'd expected her to be an enormous shitbag. And he certainly didn't think that she would follow through with the promise of sending a photo of herself. But five minutes after he hung up, he went online to check, just for the hell of it.

A message had arrived with a jpeg attachment from lizshepherd@webmail.com.

When he clicked it open, he assumed his newly met half sister was playing a strange practical joke on him. She'd sent a photo of a young Gwyneth Paltrow.

Only . . . it wasn't Gwyneth Paltrow. It was somebody who bore an uncanny resemblance to her. Except that this girl was prettier. Her eyes were brighter. Her hair was curly, but there was the same well-coifed blond sheen. She was astonishingly gorgeous. She had a smile that was somehow both goofy and sophisticated at the same time. Her skin was like cream. She wore a black sweater.

I'm related to this girl. She is a member of my immediate family.

In addition to the photo, Liz had sent an accompanying list of her vital statistics.

Name: Liz Shepherd
Age: 17
Weight: None of your business!
School: Wiltshire
Interests: Turning on and getting turned on. And reading. And dreaming.

Will didn't e-mail her back.

Instead, he turned off the computer, reached under his bed,

and chugged from the warm bottle of Smirnoff until he gasped for breath and tears rolled down his cheeks.

* * *

The five main reasons Will Shepherd believed he had been born thirty years too late:

He had the liver of a forty-nine-year-old man.

He had a sophisticated palate when it came to wines and spirits.

His musical tastes. He hated emo (whiny), techno (BO-ring), and industrial (no explanation required). He listened to Iggy and the Stooges. Alone.

He would have been the exact same age as Uncle Pete, so they could have been drinking buddies and co-conspirators and party animals and they could have gone to Stooges concerts and Vegas and orgies in the seventies, when times were loose and people weren't afraid to wear their bad habits on their sleeves.

He would have been somebody else's son.

* * *

When Will slunk into his first class, he realized he'd made *two* big mistakes. The first, of course, was that he'd opened Liz's jpeg, so for the past week he'd had to deal with the terrible knowledge of what she looked like. The second was that he'd ignored the desire to have a couple of shots of vodka for break-fast. Luckily, he could fix that mistake tomorrow. To maintain sanity, he required booze. Because when he sat down alone in the last row of seats, right next to the marble reproduction of the *Venus de Milo* (and what kind of a classroom actually displays sculpture?), he found himself staring at the following four words on the chalkboard:

LYING CHEATING STEALING SCREWING

A stodgy woman stood at the front of the room, wiping her glasses with a handkerchief. She looked like a Victorian governess.

Will assumed that she was Ms. Thompson, his comparative literature teacher. But she could have been anyone. She could have been someone's mother. He had no idea because he hadn't attended an orientation. None had been offered. No effort had been made to acquaint him with exactly what it *meant* to start at the prestigious Wiltshire School as a new senior . . . or hardly any effort, anyway. He'd received the handbook in the mail three weeks ago, but that was it.

Congratulations, the accompanying form letter had concluded, *and welcome!*

How was he supposed to feel welcome? He didn't know squat, other than the names of his teachers and the courses he was required to take. On the other hand, he supposed he should be grateful. He hadn't expected to be accepted at all. Not only had his application essay gone through several drafts and an equal number of Smirnoff liters, it had been four days late and about two thousand words too long—and one of those words was *shitbag*, repeated several times.

The kids filed into class. Will squirmed in his blazer.

Soon, very soon, Liz would come walking through that door. He kept thinking of the plastic bottle under his bed. Maybe the photo *had* been a joke. Maybe Liz weighed four hundred pounds, or was hideously deformed, or had leprosy. He watched as the stodgy woman greeted the students with sarcastic asides. "Top of the morning to *you*, Mr. Von Ristov . . . Ah, Ms. Lodge, a little groggy today, are we? . . . *Somebody* spent too much time in the sun this summer, didn't she, Ms. Broom—"

There!

Will's stomach lurched. No, no, no. Bad. The photo wasn't even flattering. In real life . . . He felt sick. Liz hurried into the room, trailed by two mildly attractive brunettes. Both were tall and somehow stylish, even in their identical uniforms. They could have been sisters. For a brief instant, Liz hesitated at the front of the class.

Her eyes zeroed in on Will's stricken face. She smiled.

The stodgy woman shut the door. "Welcome back, my young know-it-alls," she stated in a loud voice.

Someone snickered. Liz and her two friends quickly sat down in the front row.

The woman thrust a finger toward the words on the blackboard. "Can any of you tell me what *that* is?" she asked, raising her eyebrows over her glasses. "And no, the answer is not 'a concise summary of how I spent my summer, Ms. Thompson.'"

Liz and her two friends laughed.

Ms. Thompson exhaled with an exaggerated sigh. "*That*, my young know-it-alls, is what we'll be mired in for the next three months. Because those four themes—lying, cheating, stealing, and screwing—represent all that is compelling in the canon of great western literature."

The kids started cheering. Liz cheered loudest of all.

Ms. Thompson grinned in approval.

If I hadn't been born thirty years too late, I wouldn't be here right now, Will thought.

* * *

For the rest of the period, Will stared furiously into his blank notebook, struggling to ignore several large and growing concerns.

The first was that every single kid in this class knew what *vituperative* meant. (He would have to look it up when he got home.) Moreover, they had all read *Brave New World*, by Aldous Huxley, and could discuss it intelligently, and they had all vacationed in Paris, though not at the same time.

A bigger concern was that Liz and her two mildly attractive friends kept glancing over their shoulders at him and then exchanging knowing smirks.

Will would have preferred that they at least whisper. That way, they might get caught and be forced to stop.

The moment the bell rang, Will made a swift beeline for the door and hurried into the hall. He would catch up with Liz later, after lunch. He'd had the good sense to bring his fake ID, and he'd noticed an Irish pub on the walk to school this morning, McSchtink's or something—the kind of place that served vodka tonics at noon without passing judgment. Unfortunately, noon was still a good two hours away. Whatever. He could survive. Yes, because he was dropping out again tomorrow. No doubt.

His next class was algebra II. He'd never imagined he'd look forward to math class. He'd never imagined a lot of things. But at least in math, nobody would reference glamorous European capitals or obscure prizewinning novels. Or would they? Who the hell knew?

He felt a tug on his jacket.

Liz and the two girls were right behind him.

"Where do you think *you're* running off to?" Liz asked, smiling wryly.

"Uh . . ." He tried to look at the brunettes.

"These are my friends Brit Cummings and Mercedes Broomfield," Liz announced. "This is my long-lost brother, Will."

Will forced a grin. He couldn't tell who was who. Neither girl made any effort to identify herself.

"How come we've never heard of you?" one of them demanded.

"I don't know."

"Did anyone ever tell you that you look like Kevin Kline before he got old?" the other asked.

Kevin Kline? Will shook his head. He'd heard Tobey Maguire once, but even that was a stretch. He suddenly felt hot and dizzy, as if he had a high fever. "Uh, nope—"

"Come with me," Liz interrupted. She seized his arm and whisked him down the hall, away from the brunettes. "I'm so sorry," she whispered. "You have to forgive them. It's just, see, whenever they meet somebody new—and you know, somebody who they think is fairly cute—they want to make sure his face doesn't get on the site."

Will shrugged. He had no idea what to say to that. It made absolutely no sense whatsoever. Best just to keep his mouth shut.

She stopped and turned to face him. "Did you get my e-mail?"

Will nodded.

"You know about prepdate.com, don't you?"

"What-dot-com?"

Liz broke into a relieved smile. "So you don't," she breathed. "Finally. *Somebody.*" Her fingers lingered on his arm.

"What are you talking about?" Will asked. His voice cracked.

She opened her mouth—and then the bell rang. She frowned. "Listen, do you want to come to a party tonight? If you want to find out about prepdate.com, you should come."

Will stared at her. "Tonight? It's Monday. It's the first day of school."

Liz threw her head back and laughed. Apparently, he'd just told an outrageous joke. He could see the veins bulging in her slim neck.

"You're funny!" she cried. "Don't worry. It'll be chaper-oned. In a manner of speaking." She sighed. Her smile faded. "Anyway, Monday is the new Thursday. Haven't you heard?"

"Uh . . ."

"I'm kidding," Liz said.

"Oh."

Liz slung her book bag off her shoulder and yanked a scrap of paper out of a notebook. "Can I borrow your back?" she said.

"What?"

She smiled. "So I can write a number." She groaned, rolling her eyes as if she were talking to an idiot—which, for all intents and purposes, she was.

"Sure," Will said. He turned around. He felt her hands on his shoulder blades, the scribbling of a pen through the fabric of his jacket. It tickled.

"The party's at our house," Liz explained as she wrote. "Dad will be there, but don't worry. Kyle is throwing it. He really wants to meet you too. The party is for his company, prepdate.com, his so-called stroke of genius. See, he goes to this boarding school, Dorchester Prep . . . whatever. Why anyone would want to go to boarding school is beyond me. Anyway, he doesn't start until next week. The party's basically a way for him to showcase the newly upgraded site. But don't feel like you have to be in on it. He'll pressure you a lot. But you don't have to do anything you don't want. You'll be *my* guest."

She spun him around and shoved the piece of paper into his hands.

"I've got Latin," she said. "I can't believe I've finally connected with you. I've dreamed about you, you know that? But in my dreams, you never had a face. So you're much cuter in real life. Gotta run!"

She pecked him on the cheek, then dashed around the corner and vanished.

Will blinked.

The hall was empty.

Of course the hall was empty. Class had already started.

Which meant he was late for second period—on his first (and last) day of school. Well. He wasn't bound to make any whopping first impressions, anyway. He glanced at the piece of paper.

> Liz (917) 555-4672
> The party: 996 5th Ave., Apt. B, bet. 80th and 81st
> When: Tonight, 9 p.m. to whenever!
> And remember: Don't listen to Kyle. *He's* the only one who thinks he had a stroke of genius.
> Hope to see you there!
> ☺ xoxo—Liz

Hmm, Will thought. *This is completely insane.*

He wondered if Kyle was as handsome as Liz was . . . whatever she was. Nah, of course he wasn't. If Liz's twin brother was a genius, he was also probably a big geek.

chapter 2

"I'm telling you, Fat Dog, *this* is gonna be the shit."

Kyle Shepherd had made this same risky prediction many times, and he knew that if anyone else in the dorm—screw it; in the entire school—had boasted so much, Fat Dog would have long since peed in the kid's toiletries kit to shut him up. But Kyle had nothing to worry about. His ideas *were* the shit. Fat Dog worshiped him. With good reason: Fat Dog had netted over four hundred dollars from Kyle's last scheme, the already-legendary "Help the Heroes!" campaign. And this new one had the potential to bring in serious CEO-style cash money, for the simple reason that it promised sex.

Kyle pushed away from his computer so that Fat Dog could

lean in and get a better look. The screen was blank—a tabula rasa (the presentation was more dramatic that way)—except for a single name: prepdate.com.

"Cool font," Fat Dog whispered. He reeked of meat loaf.

For a moment, Kyle had a vivid fantasy of strapping Fat Dog's pale two hundred pounds into a dental chair and squeezing an entire tube of toothpaste down his throat.

Being an ass kisser was one thing. Being an ass kisser with bad breath and proximity problems doomed Fat Dog to a future that was too depressing to think about. (And what self-respecting junior ate the meat loaf they dished out in the dining hall, anyway?) But he was a good programmer, and Kyle knew that he couldn't pull this off without him.

"How did you think this up?" Fat Dog asked.

"How do you think, bro?" Kyle said. "Surfing the web late at night."

Fat Dog didn't say anything.

"Alone," Kyle added. "Just me and the computer."

"Yeah, but how?"

Oh, come on! Take a jab at me! Kyle had left the door wide open. Anyone else at Dorchester would have walked right through it. When somebody confessed to surfing the web alone at night, you accused that somebody of jacking off. It was an unwritten law. You didn't even have to be clever about it. ("So where's the box of Kleenex?" Or, "I think electrolysis can take care of those hairy palms.") Kyle was a little annoyed, actually. You try to throw a kid a bone; you try to establish a little rapport, some mutual respect . . . but it was best not to get too worked up about these things. Besides, if Fat Dog had been hanging out with anybody else, he probably *would* have taken a jab. Ever since "Help the Heroes!" though, his behavior around Kyle had been twitchy at best.

"Think about it, bro," Kyle said. "It's a natural extension of an already-burgeoning subculture, right?"

"What subculture is that?"

"The subculture of the public loser. The people who aren't afraid to say, 'Yes, I am that desperate. I am *so* desperate that I am willing to post my face on the web or go on a reality show because I pray that somebody out there will be horny enough to have sex with me. Or at least give me a blow job. Anybody! Please!!!'"

Fat Dog's face reddened. He tried to laugh.

"I can't believe that somebody hasn't thought of this already," Kyle said. He shoved Fat Dog out of the way and moved back to his desk, then clicked over to the web. "I mean, it's so obvious. Check this out."

A list of sites flashed across the screen: match.com, nerve.com, friendster . . . the search engine listed one to twenty out of a possible 81,063.

"See, there are dating services for every possible segment of society," Kyle explained. "Lesbian seniors. Bondage freaks. Militant threesomes . . . and they can all post personals for each other—except the richest, horniest segment of all."

Fat Dog blinked at him. "Who's that?"

"*Us*, you asshole."

"Oh."

Fat Dog sat on the edge of Kyle's bed. In the dim glow of the Tiffany desk lamp, he looked like a flesh-colored beach ball with a blazer draped over it.

Kyle's room was always somewhat dark because he refused to use the dorm's built-in fluorescent lights. The vibe was too ghoulish. The desk lamp's mellow, old-time speakeasy vibe made it much easier to scam on chicks. Kyle had even duct-taped the switch on the wall to keep prospective scams (and Fat Dog) from accidentally turning on the overhead. Unfortunately, no female had entered his room in over four months. And in truth, the last one—Marjorie Howe, a.k.a. "the Jam Band Slut"— looked ghoulish no matter what the lighting.

Fat Dog smiled again, but his jowls were creased. "You want me to set up a dating service for kids our age. That's what this is about, right?"

"Not just *any* kids our age," Kyle explained. "The over-privileged. The unsupervised. The horn dogs with the seven-figure trust funds, the ones who go to the Gold and Silver Ball looking to get laid. The kids who spot some chick just as she's leaving the Waldorf and are like, 'Man, I wish she went to Dorchester, but she doesn't. So how can I get with her? If only there were some sort of database for single prep school chicks. She must go to Exeter or Hotchkiss or *something*, right?'"

Fat Dog's face was blank.

"Don't you get it?" Kyle said. "Every prep school bro wants to find that new, perfect chick—the chick who doesn't go to their school. But they would never go to a cheesy online dating service to find her. And if they did sink to that level, they'd want the whole thing to be *classy*. They'd want it to be exclusive—like a social club, with a screening process and membership fees. They would *pay* for it because that way, they wouldn't feel like public losers, like volunteers or contestants. See what I'm saying?"

Fat Dog seemed concerned.

"What?" Kyle demanded.

"Are you sure this is legal?"

"Why wouldn't it be?"

"It's just that, ah . . . see, if you're going to, like, solicit money from minors—you know, people under eighteen—the law requires that their parents sign a consent form."

"Really?" Kyle said. "Are you sure?"

Fat Dog nodded. "Positive."

"How do you know? You sound like F. Lee Butthead over here. I mean, no offense, but you haven't passed the bar exam in your spare time, right?"

"No, but . . ." Fat Dog lowered his voice and cast a furtive glance toward the closed door. "See, remember when we were doing the 'Help the Heroes!' thing?"

Kyle rolled his eyes. *Jesus.* Fat Dog still felt the need to whisper whenever "Help the Heroes!" came up. He had to get over it already. They hadn't done anything *wrong*. On the contrary: Kyle saw the two of them (well, himself mostly; it had been his idea) as the biggest philanthropists he knew. Who else had organized a campuswide relief effort for widows of fallen soldiers in the War on Terror? Who else had thought of such a sacrificial, heartbreaking campaign? Who else had worked like a fiend to raise $32,561.04—in less than three months? Nobody. Not even the faculty. Of course not. Nobody gave a crap about the war, except selfishly ("When will fanatics attack us again?") or in the abstract ("Shouldn't we be doing more to understand these fanatics?"). Yet amid the lameness and apathy, Kyle alone had maintained the focus, the *leadership* needed to rally the school around a righteous cause—one that had in fact briefly served as both inspiration and salve for the entire Dorchester community (right-wing jackasses and wimpy knee-jerk liberals alike). *He* was the hero.

And okay, sure, maybe he and Fat Dog had pocketed a little loose change in the process. But feel guilty about that? Why? Because they hadn't told anyone? Big deal. It wasn't like they were *embezzling*. Everybody who'd donated money knew that a tiny percentage of it would go toward maintaining the "Help the Heroes!" web site (Fat Dog's job) and overseeing the distribution of funds (Kyle's). These were no easy tasks. No, sir. Kyle had *earned* a fee. And it was a meager fee to boot: he'd taken only about three grand for himself. Out of over thirty-two.

"What's your point, Fat Dog?" he asked.

"It's just that I came across this same legal issue before with . . . you know, the other thing. And I'm not sure parents would, like, um, consent to let their kids join a dating service that they have to pay for. I mean, a charity is different, you know? Parents want their kids to do that."

"Yeah, but they would want their kids to do this too. We're talking about Dorchester parents. We're talking about the ones who'd go ballistic if their sons hooked up with any chick who couldn't trace her roots back to the *Mayflower*. Remember what happened to Harrison Shaw? You want that to happen to you?"

"I guess not," Fat Dog mumbled.

"You mean of course not," Kyle said with a grin. You didn't mess with what happened to Harrison Shaw. It was like Greek tragedy. Worse. It was like part of the Bible: one of those epic Dorchester myths that had somehow, with the passage of three years' time, made the transition from apocrypha to gospel. Even *he* had started to believe that it might have actually happened.

Harrison Shaw was a senior when Kyle and Fat Dog were freshmen. Not just any senior, either: tall, blond, skinny, rich as hell . . . a lot like Kyle, actually. The ladies loved him. He could have had his pick of the litter. But for some reason, he had a Latina fetish. His father, who was no fan of nonwhites, hated him for it. ("I'm not a bigot," Mr. Shaw was rumored to have once said. "I just don't trust those people.")

The situation came to a boil that Thanksgiving, when Mr. Shaw found his son in their pool house with a fifteen-year-old Colombian girl. Mr. Shaw yanked Harrison out of Dorchester and sent him to the Fenton Military Academy to straighten him out. But there was no stopping El Conquistador. Three days after Harrison started at Fenton, he snuck home. Within hours he was seducing Maria, the Shaw family's new twenty-two-year-old Dominican maid.

This time, his stepmom caught him—buck-ass naked with Maria in the walk-in shoe closet. And as if that weren't traumatic enough, Harrison's stepmom *loved* Maria. She'd insisted on hiring the woman despite protests from her hubby, who "[didn't] trust those people." So she freaked. She cracked a Ch'ing vase over Harrison's head. The blow turned him into a special-needs case. (From then on, he refused to talk to anyone except Bunny, his stuffed giraffe.) Mr. Shaw divorced the step-mom and sued her for $100 million in damages. And the whole mess could have been avoided if Harrison had simply followed his father's advice and scammed on their neighbor's daughter, Faith Cushing, who had hideous acne but also "a great person-ality" and the right lineage.

Or so the myth went.

"You know, you're right," Fat Dog said. "I think most prep school parents *would* pay for a matchmaking service for their kids."

Kyle nodded. "Of course they would. We'll make it parent-friendly. We'll get them involved, so that finding a perfect match will become a family affair. I mean, picture it, bro: You and your dad are sitting together at the computer over spring break. You're searching for that perfect chick. Then this hottie's face pops up on the screen. And your dad is like, 'Wait, that's my business partner's daughter! I *love* her!' And her quote is like: 'Hi, I'm Piper! I'm a Sagittarius, and I'm looking for a big fat guy with a big fat heart—the kind of guy who would design a patriotic web site for fallen soldiers in the War on Terror!' Boom. Done. Two days later, you're in her pants."

Fat Dog stared at him. "You're sick."

"I'm a fucking genius."

"Yeah, but still. I don't know."

"What's not to know? I'm talking romance. Everybody loves romance."

"You're talking sex."

"You say tomato; I say tah-mah-toe. True love is just a double click away."

Fat Dog laughed. "That sounds like an ad slogan."

"Holy shit, you're right."

Kyle stared into space, his eyes narrowing. He suddenly saw the whole thing before him, *the entire marketing strategy*—with an emphasis on first love, *puppy* love, and Hallmark-style testimonials from chicks: "I first met [place boy's name here] at etiquette camp five years ago. I thought I'd never see him again. But when Daddy helped me join prepdate.com™ and I saw his face on the web, I just melted. Now we have plans to go to Dartmouth together in the fall. . . ."

Yeah, that would be a deal-closer with any prep school parent. *True love is just a double click away.* Jesus, that was brilliant! And it just *came* to him!

"What?" Fat Dog asked.

"Nothing." Adrenaline coursed through Kyle's veins, warm and euphoric, like a shot of Jägermeister. "So when do we get started?"

"I don't know, Kyle. I mean—"

"Look, bro, this time, we'll split the profits straight down the middle, fifty-fifty. Okay? People are gonna *love* this. Trust me. Plus, it's coming from *us*. The 'Help the Heroes!' guys. We're *saints*, as far as everyone is concerned. We just gotta pitch it and market it in the right terms. Like we're serving a higher purpose. Like we're forging lifelong relationships."

Fat Dog didn't say anything.

"What are you worried about?" Kyle asked.

"Nothing, I guess . . ."

"Right. So how long do you think it'll take to get the site up and running?"

"I don't know," Fat Dog said. "Maybe two weeks? We'll have to file a bunch of forms, too. I mean, if we plan on running a business for profit."

Kyle smiled and patted Fat Dog's shoulder. "Don't sweat it. Your dad can help you with that legal stuff, right? In the meantime, I'll start spreading the word. I'll get all the bros on board. And don't worry about the consent issue. I know everybody's parents will go for this. Trust me."

The more he listened to himself talk, the more intoxicated he grew. People were going to freak over this! *Everybody.* Yeah . . . come to think of it, there was probably only one bro at Dorchester whose parents would refuse to pay or consent to have their son sign up for prepdate.com, and that was Kyle himself.

But Kyle's parents didn't really count. For anything.

chapter 3

When Will arrived at 996 Fifth Avenue, he started laughing. Not that there was anything remotely funny about the situation. No. He'd seen the place maybe a dozen times before, on field trips to the Met or the occasional drunken jaunt into Central Park, and he'd wondered . . . but he'd always told himself: *Nah, it couldn't be.* He'd just assumed Dad lived in the adjacent building, the normal building—the one with the awning, the one that probably housed a dozen typical, fabulous, pre-war apartments, the kind of apartments in which any run-of-the-mill millionaire would live.

He'd assumed wrong.

The awning building was 996–998 Fifth Avenue, one of those weird New York City double addresses. It must have been connected to Dad's building somehow, but Mom had never clarified the exact architectural relationship for him. Nor had Uncle Pete. Not that Will had asked or even cared. There had been no reason to care. Mom pretty much refused to travel west of Park Avenue or north of Seventy-second Street, so they'd never been up this way together anyway.

Now Will was beginning to understand why.

Nine ninety-six Fifth Avenue was a palace. No exaggeration. It was built of gray stone, maybe six stories tall, with gargoyles and chimneys and ornate cornices, something straight out of Vienna or Prague (not that Will had ever been), particularly dazzling when illuminated by the streetlamps at night . . . and there were only two silver buttons on the buzzer: A and B. Which probably meant that there were only two residences—*in the whole entire place*.

And one of them was Dad's.

Will stopped laughing.

So here he was.

I am about to see my father in person for the first time in eighteen years.

It was a breezy, late summer night. He was entering Dad's home. There was something Tragic about it—tragic with a capital *T*; *epic*, really, in the vein of Aeschylus or Shakespeare or *The O.C.* Especially since Liz was in there. Kyle too. It was a "major turning point," as Wiltshire would phrase it. But Will felt nothing. Well, almost nothing. He kept thinking about that Danish he'd eaten this afternoon at the deli on Seventy-ninth and

Third, how spongy and bland it had been: able to absorb the vodka tonics he'd had for lunch but unable to provoke any sensation worth describing.

That Danish was his brain right now.

Of course, he'd had three Jack and Cokes before coming here. He probably should have only had two. Still, Mom was meeting with a client, and when Mom went out to meet with a client, the laws of the universe dictated that the contents of her liquor cabinet were up for grabs. Oh, yes. They most certainly did. And a person did not defy the laws of the universe. *Poor Mom.* What if her meeting got canceled and she came home?

Will hadn't mustered the courage to tell her what he was really doing tonight. She probably thought he was back in their sad little two-bedroom, watching *Law & Order* reruns. What could he have said, though? That he'd embarked on an epic voyage: that the abandoned son was going to face the enormous shitbag—finally, after all these years? And *why*? How could he have explained it? *"Uh, Mom, my half sister invited me to this party for my half brother's web site. . . ."* Sure. That would go over really well. Mom would have put in an emergency call to Dr. Brown. Which might be a wise idea, come to think of it.

He glanced at his watch. Nine twenty-two. Right on time. He squinted through gaps in the gilded wrought-iron protective door. He saw a lobby, but he couldn't really make out anything besides a big chandelier.

He pressed button B.

Seconds later, there was a loud *bzzzzt.*

Will tugged on the doorknob. It budged a half inch at most.

He had to use both hands. He winced a little, throwing his back into the effort. By the time he staggered inside, he was breathless. The door slammed behind him: *THWAP!* There was a spiral staircase at the far end of the lobby. Will also noticed an unmarked door on the left. A giant porcelain urn sat beside it. Man. The size of that thing . . . It was bigger than a garbage can. This wasn't a palace; it was a museum. *Now what?*

In answer to his question, the door opened—

And there he was.

Dad. The enormous shitbag. Forrest Shepherd II.

There were options, Will knew. Step forward; shake hands. Burst into tears. Hug the man. Strangle him and leave the corpse in a messy heap beside the giant urn, then bolt. *Step forward, step forward. . . . At least I should do that.*

Dad looked a hell of a lot worse in person than he did in his latest photo. Granted, the photo was ten years old. But he was more grizzled and disheveled and noticeably fatter. His beard was stringy. He wore a checkered flannel shirt. One of the flaps was untucked. His graying blond hair was pulled back in a ponytail. His blue eyes were glassy. He looked as if he had absolutely no business being in this neighborhood, let alone this house. Then again, Will didn't either.

"You're Will, right?" Dad finally said.

"I am," Will replied.

How many times had Will envisioned this confrontation? More than he should have. Recurring fantasies had swept him up in fiery embraces over the years—generally whenever Dad's name came up or whenever Mom had a particularly bad day, which often went hand in hand. Will would clench his fists at his sides, thinking all the worst things he could possibly think . . . And now the fantasies came flooding back to him, like the time when he was ten years old, the day Mom's favorite and most lucrative client had left her—some portrait artist named Ari— and she'd broken down at the kitchen table and wailed: "Everyone leaves me! Your father, Ari, all of them!" Will, with his ten-year-old logic, had thought: *She wouldn't be crying if Dad hadn't left us first. So maybe I should just go kill him. I can shove a stupid paintbrush down his stupid throat and burn down his house.* . . . But he hadn't, of course. He'd just stood with his fists at his sides. And here was history repeating itself, in this antiseptic lobby.

Once again, part of him screamed for a response, one that would turn all that disturbing fantasy into action-thriller-bloodshed TRIUMPH!!!

Dad offered a faint smile. "You can come in if you want."

Will glided toward the apartment. Options, options, options . . . The handshake? The hug? The smile? The strangulation? His feet moved, but his mind and limbs had officially ended their fuzzy communication for the night. He might as well have ridden on a conveyor belt. He kept his eyes fixed on Dad's exposed shirt flap.

"I wasn't sure if you were gonna make it," Dad said.

"Neither was I," Will said.

Dad hesitated. He fiddled with his beard. He, too, seemed to be weighing the options. The paternal clasping of the shoulders? The apology? The eye contact? Instead, Dad turned his back on

Will and gestured inside—then shut the door behind both of them, effectively ruling out intimacy, period.

Will found himself in a dim marble corridor, wedged between a lacquered side table and a thuggish kid in oversized jeans and a black wool cap. The kid's skin was deathly pale, almost blue. He glared at Will, who in turn stared at his feet. Cocktail party noises drifted toward them. Will realized that he was standing very near a bathroom, because he also heard the unmistakable sound of a stream of urine, accompanied by the abundant passing of gas.

"Well, Ricky," Dad said. "That ought to take care of our business for tonight."

"Whatever, G," the kid grunted.

Will felt a tap on his shoulder.

He glanced up. The bathroom door was indeed less than five feet away.

"Aren't you going to introduce yourself?" Dad asked, frowning at him.

"What do you mean?" Will said.

"This is Ricky," Dad said. He patted the blue-faced kid's back. "He's a local entrepreneur. Just like my boy, Kyle."

The kid shoved his nose within inches of Will's.

"Whaddup, *bee-yatch*!" he bellowed. His breath smelled like McDonald's. He burst into a wide smile, revealing a mouthful of yellow teeth. "I'm just playin', yo."

Before Will could respond, the kid threw open the door and strode from the hall.

"Stay black, Ricky!" Dad called after him.

The kid didn't answer.

Dad sighed. "Ah, Ricky," he said. "What a nut." He gently closed the door. Then he reached into his shirt pocket and pulled out a tiny glass vial, pinching it between his thumb and forefinger. "Feel like a little toot?" he asked. He unscrewed the vial's cap and tapped out a small pile of white powder on the side table: *click, click*.

Will's eyes narrowed.

"Don't worry," Dad said. "It's all right. I just need a little pick-me-up. My coffee machine's busted."

From inside the bathroom, the sound of a flushing toilet replaced the sounds of peeing and farting. Will found a tremendous degree of comfort in that. He shifted on his feet.

"Don't be so nervous," Dad chided.

"I haven't seen you since I was an infant," Will said.

"Yeah, but I'm like wine, kiddo. I don't get older. I *age*."

A faucet squeaked. The bathroom door flew open. A spindly, middle-aged woman in a long black dress—a vague clone of the Wicked Witch of the West from *The Wizard of Oz*, minus the cone hat—stepped out and quickly shut the door behind her. Her face was thin and humorless. She sneered at Dad.

"At it again, Forrest?" she said.

"That's right," he replied. "There's nothing wrong with a healthy stress reliever."

The woman arched an eyebrow and strolled down the corridor. Her high heels clattered on the marble floor. "It's your heart," she said, without turning around. "If you want it to fail, that's your prerogative."

"Yeah, and that's what I say about your digestive tract. Judging from what I just heard in there, those herbal supplements aren't helping."

The woman raised a middle finger over her shoulder. "Please tell your young drug dealer friend to get lost," she said, vanishing around the corner.

Dad winked at Will. "She thinks you're Ricky," he whispered. He jammed his right forefinger against his right nostril and leaned directly over the pile of white powder, snorting all of it in one long inhalation. As soon as he finished, he straightened up and licked his teeth. "That's my wife, in case you were wondering," he said, holding his breath. "She and I often disagree on the definition of health."

Health? Actually, Will had to admit: his own definition of health was shaky at best. For example, he needed Jack and Coke number four right now. It was, in fact, essential for his health. He imagined that his liver had become a character on a children's show: *Will's Zany Liver*. The character was like Cookie Monster from *Sesame Street*. Only instead of being a cute little Muppet who went crazy for cookies, Will's Zany Liver was a bloated little organ that went crazy for booze.

"Hey, could I get something to drink?" Will asked.

"First things first," Dad said. "Have you gotten your driver's license yet?"

Will shook his head. "No. Not yet."

"Not yet?" Dad sniffed. "What are you waiting for, a written invitation from the DMV? Let me ask you something else. Do you know why you got into Wiltshire?"

"Actually, no." Will wondered what it would feel like to smash his fist into Dad's runny nose. It would probably hurt his knuckles. It might be messy, too. "I have no idea. That's a good question."

"Well, I read your application essay," Dad said. "Funny stuff. Very *Heartbreaking Work of Staggering Genius*. The footnotes were a nice touch."

Will knew that he should respond with something—shock, embarrassment, indignation. Weren't those essays confidential? But all he could think about was that tall Jack and Coke. Will's Zany Liver was up to its usual wacky high jinks. Watch out, kids! Hide your whiskey! He's a-comin'!

"They didn't believe that you were my son," Dad went on, speaking more quickly. "I mean, you referred to me as an 'enormous shitbag'"—he made shaky air quotes—"what was it . . . four times?" He laughed. "You've got a flair for prose."

I'm trapped, Will thought.

"Anyway, I assured them that yes, I *was* an enormous shitbag, but that they shouldn't hold that against *you*. And then I offered to donate some cash. That eased their pain. I like to *give*, man. Ever since I was your age. Wanna hear a story? If you think your uncle Pete was a radical, check this out: It's the summer of seventy-one. The West Village. Barrow Street. Barrow and Commerce. Rents were cheaper back then. All these self-proclaimed 'commies,' hanging out in a little studio apartment. The dark side of the liberal arts education. We start rapping about how we're gonna 'strike a blow against the military-industrial complex.' So we decide to pool some money together and send an anonymous donation to the Vietcong. The sum was close to thirty large. Worst money we ever spent. It probably wound up subsidizing Vietnamese hookers. If it even got that far. Live and learn, though, right? A few years later, I start sponsoring Vietnamese war orphans . . . paying for them to come here, setting them up with adoptive families, taking care of their schooling, whatever. The punch line? Most of those orphans now work for the military-industrial complex—"

"There you are!"

Liz appeared from out of nowhere. She swept down the corridor and looped her hand under Will's arm.

"I thought I heard the doorbell ring," she said.

Thank you, Lord. In spite of his better instincts, Will grinned stupidly.

Liz was still wearing her blue Wiltshire uniform. She'd pulled her shiny blond curls back in a bun. Her cheeks were pink.

She glanced at Dad. "Are you two catching up?"

Dad's jaw began to grind. "I gotta take a dump," he said. He hurried into the bathroom and slammed the door.

Liz frowned. "Thanks for the update." She looked at Will. "Are you all right?"

He took a deep breath. "That's a funny question," he managed.

"I guess it is. I'm sorry!" She giggled and dragged him out of the corridor and up a dark, carpeted stairwell. Will stumbled after her. "The party is up here," she said. "Kyle didn't believe you were coming. He's gonna be so psyched."

"Hey, can I ask you something?" Will said.

"Of course."

"Is your mom a Wiccan?"

"A Wiccan?" Liz seemed puzzled. "I don't know. What does that mean, exactly?"

"Um . . . somebody who believes in the occult and practices magic?"

"Oh. Maybe. I know she mail-orders a lot of weird health food. And she talks a lot about something called 'the SPIRIT.' All caps. Can I ask *you* something?"

"Sure."

"Was Dad doing coke?"

"I think he was," Will said.

"I figured. He always starts talking about the Vietcong when he does coke."

At the top of the stairs, Liz escorted Will into what could have been a wing of the New York Public Library. The room was opulent, massive . . . lined with books and exotic bric-a-brac, crawling with cocktail-bearing caterers—and with kids his age too, a lot of whom he thought he recognized from Wiltshire. Several of them were huddled around a tall kid with blond hair who sat at a *Godfather*-style desk near the door, fiddling with a sleek laptop. One of the crowd caught Will's eye: an obese, babyish boy in a four-button black Armani suit, who was staring straight at Liz. He looked to be all of thirteen. He tapped the blond kid and whispered in his ear. The blond kid turned toward them.

"Yo, Liz! You got a new one for me?"

Liz rolled her eyes. "No, Kyle. This is Will. Remember?"

"Will? Fuck! You actually came?"

And now I'm leaving. Will swayed on his feet. He clenched his fists at his sides so tightly that he worried he might have a seizure. *Get out. Get out.* Back to the sad little two-bedroom and the *Law & Order* reruns. Yes. Definitely. Immediately.

Seeing Dad was traumatic enough. And Will supposed he'd known all along that his half brother wasn't going to be the big geek he'd been praying for. But he'd never imagined that Kyle would belong in an Aryan Nations recruiting brochure, either. Unlike Dad, he'd come a long way from the *Cats* photo. He sort of reminded Will of Brandon Farkas, that guy from S——with the ice blue eyes and pentagram tattoo on his forearm, the guy who called himself "the Killer" and insisted everyone else do the same. ("Ain't nobody gonna mess with the Killer," he would proclaim. "'Less they wanna get kilt.") On the plus side, Kyle wasn't a male version of Gwyneth Paltrow. He had the same narrow nose as Liz, but that was it.

"Will Shepherd," Kyle said. "I can't believe it. Wait, you *do* go by Shepherd, don't you?"

"I do," Will said. He tried to ignore the curious stares. So. The family reunion was complete. *Mental note: Start taking meds again. Also, ask Dr. Brown why brain always short-circuits and makes me talk like a retard during "major turning points."*

"Hey, sorry about your uncle," Kyle said. He grinned. "So, you wanna get laid?"

"What?"

Everybody in the room burst out laughing.

"Be nice," Liz said.

"What's nicer than getting laid?" Kyle grumbled. "It's a party, Liz." He turned back to the computer. "I've been looking forward to meeting you, Will. Well, not really. I've never thought about it. But tonight we can celebrate. See, we've been trying to get my sister to put her face on the site for the past four months, ever since her boyfriend dumped her. Damon. He sort of looks like Hugh Grant. Gwyneth and Hugh, they used to call them. His dad is thinking about buying stock in my company. The shit is blowing up, bro. You better get in on it. I've gotten over four hundred hits on the site today."

"You mean *we've* gotten over four hundred hits," the obese guy said.

"I know, Fat Dog." Kyle smiled again. "*We* had over four hundred hits." He raised a hand. The obese kid gave him a high five.

Will started backing toward the stairwell.

"Anyway, she finally agreed to get in on the action," Kyle said.

"Yeah, but I'm already having second thoughts," Liz added.

"Really?" the obese kid said. "Bummer."

"Easy there, Fat Dog," Kyle muttered. "So, Will, how much do you know about Liz?" He didn't look up once as he spoke. His eyes were fixed on the computer, as if connected to it by a string. "Probably not a lot, right? I mean, seeing as you just met her today? Let me give you the inside scoop. See, the

thing about my twin sister . . . She suffered some major disappointments this summer. You know why?" He paused,
clicking the mouse a few times. "She thinks she's an adult
stuck in a teenager's body. The way I see it, she needs to let
loose and chill out a little. *That's* her problem. And hopefully
prepdate.com can help."

"I can hear you, Kyle," Liz said. "I'm in the room, remember?"

"Yeah, I was wondering where that stink was coming from,"
Kyle said.

"You want a drink?" Liz whispered to Will.

He shook his head violently. "Nah. I should be on my way."

Liz grabbed two plastic cups of champagne off a passing
tray. "Come on, just one drink. Kyle is nervous, that's all. He
was really looking forward to this. I promise."

Will snatched a cup from her and downed the whole thing in
less than three seconds. His throat burned. He hadn't gotten
drunk on champagne in—how long? He was pretty sure the last
time was at an opening for one of his mom's second-tier
clients, a three-hundred-pound Sikh named Raj Javjani. Raj
made collages out of junk mail. Will learned later that he was a
mailman. But the opening had been fun. . . . Not that Will
remembered much of it. He only knew that he'd felt like death
the next day, and that he'd blacked out, and that he needed to
black out right now, too. At least for the next two minutes,
before he ran home.

Home. Right. That was almost funny.

"Whoa there, cowboy!" Liz exclaimed.

Almost instantly, Will felt a pleasant fire deep inside his belly. It began to spread in slow waves up toward his head.

"How about another?" Liz suggested.

Will blinked and rubbed his eyes. "Keep 'em coming," he gasped.

chapter 4

For the record: Liz Shepherd did *not* think of herself as an adult trapped in a teenager's body. Her parents were teenagers trapped in adult bodies—*that* was the problem. (Or one of the problems.) Another problem was Damon. He'd dumped her because she was "too uptight." But he didn't understand her. He didn't understand what it was like to have an absentee mother and a father who was more interested in eating gourmet falafel, doing drugs, and espousing ludicrous conspiracy theories than he was in raising his own children. And when you had parents like that, you had to take a certain amount of responsibility for yourself. So if that made you "uptight" . . .

The biggest problem, though, was that Damon thought that Liz's parents were somehow cool.

He wasn't the only one. All of Liz's friends "dug" her parents. (And who says "dug," anyway?) If she had to hear one more story about how funny Dad was when he "sparked a bowl, *dude*," or "downloaded a Grateful Dead bootleg, *dude*" . . . No, the only thing to "dig" about Dad was his '88 Volvo, a lovable old heap of junk he kept in Miami, which Liz was certain she'd inherit upon her graduation. But *que sera, sera*. You dealt with life's cruel gags as best you could. Her twin brother had dealt with them by becoming a web-based crook. Liz, however, refused to wallow in either slime or self-pity.

Instead, she decided to intern at a publishing company.

* * *

The idea came to her in May, when she rented *Almost Famous*. She'd heard that the movie was based on a true story. She'd heard from Dad (when wasted, but still) that Cameron Crowe, the director, had written articles for *Rolling Stone* when he was just fifteen years old—simply because he'd had the courage to submit a sample and the talent to land himself a gig. At twenty-two, Cameron Crowe had already written and directed his first movie. Or so she'd read in his online celebrity bio.

Well, Liz figured that she was probably just as literate as anybody her age. She *loved* to read. And most people her age wanted to be writers. But she was going to flip it. She was going to be an editor. A famous one, too. Why not? Maxwell Perkins was famous. Besides, people got famous for all sort of ridiculous things these days. She knew she had the eye to spot a great book in the works. After all, she'd been the very first girl in her third-grade class ever to read *Alice in Wonderland*. All she needed was a head start.

Yes. Her summer was going to rule.

Not only would a publishing internship help take her mind off Damon (whose only real selling point, frankly, was a passing resemblance to Hugh Grant), but it would also look great on her college applications, *and* she could work part-time through all of senior year, making valuable contacts for the future. She couldn't lose. Sure, maybe she wouldn't be able to spend as much time with Brit or Mercedes as she would have liked. But that was a small price to pay. Let them shop and tan themselves into the first stages of melanoma. She was moving ahead.

* * *

Unfortunately, after combing newspapers and the web for most of May, Liz discovered that the only available summer internship was at Empire Books.

Empire's biggest claim to fame was a lowbrow series of unauthorized celebrity biographies called The Dirty Dish. As if that weren't sketchy enough, the internship was in the mass-market young adult division, the part of the company that cranked out dozens of cheesy teen romance novels a year (with titles like *Boy Toys!*), as well as creepy horror books for boys who would probably grow up to be public masturbators.

I might as well intern for Hustler, she thought sadly.

On the plus side, it paid seven bucks an hour. Most

internships didn't pay at all. And if any of her friends or teachers ever asked, she could always say that she'd interned in "children's literature" (immediately evoking images of *Alice in Wonderland* or, at worst, *Harry Potter*), and it wouldn't be a lie. Not technically.

So Liz swallowed her pride and took it. She had to start somewhere.

And big surprise: at first, everything seemed great—much cooler than she expected. The office *itself* was cool, stuffed into a sunny loft in the Flatiron District. She'd also assumed she'd be working with a bunch of overweight, middle-aged perverts. Not so. The mass-market young adult crew reminded her of the on-air personalities at MTV2: witty and stylish and self-deprecating—like Ned Parrish, the twenty-six-year-old GBNG (gay-but-not-gay) editor who claimed that he really *wasn't* an editor. He was a singer/songwriter. His true goal in life was to be "the next Beck, because he's as bad a guitarist as I am." Editing teen pulp was just a way to pay the rent.

"Welcome to the armpit of the publishing industry," he said to Liz as she settled into her cubicle the very first day. "Now, let me ask you something. Do you think that selling a children's book called *Doing It 24/7!* will land you an eternity in hell? If not, you're in the right place. From now on, your motto is 'Pure schlock and proud of it!'"

That set the tone. Right off the bat, Liz felt as if she were part of a big, inside joke. Nobody ever treated her like an intern. Nobody ever asked her to get coffee. They only rarely told her to make Xerox copies. Most importantly, they asked for her opinions. She was barely older than their target readership. They told her that she was "tuned in." Their vibe was so hip, so glamorous-but-not-glamorous, so mature.

In fact, in those first heady days, there was only one person at Empire who got on Liz's nerves, and that was her boss—Carol Whitehead, a plastic surgery casualty who bore an uncanny resemblance to that Rolling Stones guitarist . . . Ron What's-his-name, the one with the mullet. (Liz had been forced to gaze upon Ron and the other Stones every day for years on end, as Dad had insisted upon framing his signed *Voodoo Lounge* tour poster and mounting it in the upstairs kitchen.)

Carol Whitehead repeated herself constantly. Worse, she used words like *zeitgeist* in conversation.

"Remember, we have to find a way to do *American Idol* in book form!" she liked to yell across the office. "We have to redefine the zeitgeist, people!"

But Liz just figured that you were supposed to detest your boss, the same way that you were supposed to detest your parents. It was par for the course. Still . . . Liz felt sort of bad for her. Talk about a high-strung bundle of insecurity. She was worse than the girls at Wiltshire. Plus—and this was the sad part—she didn't wear a wedding ring, even though she was married. *Poor woman.* You just knew she hadn't gotten laid in years.

* * *

The trouble began one afternoon in July.

Carol Whitehead summoned the entire division away from their cubicles to an "emergency brainstorming session." She needed their help in creating a clever pun to use as an advertising tagline for Empire's newest children's thriller, *Killer Rabbits*.

The plot of *Killer Rabbits*: A mad scientist named Dr. Zane creates a breed of super-intelligent bunnies. But the experiment goes horribly wrong. The fuzzy little guys turn out to be evil (duh, cloning?) and they tear Dr. Zane to shreds. So it's up to his assistants—two wacky teenagers named Horton and Sue—to stop them. In fewer than a hundred pages, a series of predictable twists suddenly climaxes in a frenzied bloodbath, Horton and Sue exchange a G-rated smooch, and then the book is over.

Okay. It wasn't exactly Lewis Carroll. But what was?

Anyway, Liz couldn't help but notice how pleased Carol Whitehead looked as she sat there at the head of the conference table, waiting for her staff. Liz exchanged a glance with Ned Parrish. *She's already come up with a tagline*, Liz thought—and clearly Ned Parrish was thinking the same thing. *She only called the meeting to prove to the rest of us how brilliant she is. Classic.*

Sure enough, as soon as everyone was seated, Carol Whitehead stood. "Okay, people, I have the perfect tagline," she said. She paused dramatically, then announced, beaming: "So bunny, I forgot to laugh!"

Nobody beamed back.

"So bunny, I forgot to laugh!" she said again.

A period of strained silence followed.

She scowled and sat down.

Suddenly, a bolt of inspiration struck Liz out of nowhere. Well, actually it struck while she was staring at Carol Whitehead's Ron-Wood-style mullet.

"How about, 'Ever had a really bad *hare* day?'" Liz said. "You know, *h-a-r-e*?"

Everybody started cracking up.

"Genius!" Ned Parrish yelled. "Give that girl a raise!"

Liz blushed.

Carol Whitehead faked a smile. Yes, Liz's idea was impressive, especially for someone so young and inexperienced. Meeting adjourned.

And so it happened: Liz's slogan appeared the following Thursday on the promotional materials for the series.

KILLER RABBITS™
EVER HAD A REALLY BAD HARE DAY?

Oh my God, I've been published, Liz thought when she saw it, and she'd never felt giddier. *I'm a seventeen-year-old intern, and I've been published. Just like Cameron Crowe. This could be it! This could be that first crazy, unpredictable step on the golden ladder to happiness.* The *Larry King* interview, five years from now:

> Larry: *You've changed the face of publishing—pretty remarkable for somebody who's only twenty-two. How did you get your start?*
>
> Liz: *You're never going to believe this.* (Embarrassed laughter.) *By interning in the mass-market young adult division of Empire Books.*

Larry: *You're right. I don't believe it.*

Liz: *No, no, I swear!* (More laughter.)

Larry: *Empire? You mean those purveyors of teen smut?*

Liz: *The very same.*

* * *

The next morning, Carol Whitehead dropped by Liz's cubicle.

"You're doing a great job, Liz," she said. "But I have to be honest. We're making some changes around here. I'm sure you're old enough to know that Empire isn't worth what it used to be. Our stock is down. Children's fiction is going more literary. Mass-market paperbacks are out. We have to roll with the times. *We* have to go more literary. From now on, I'll be aggressively pushing hardcover novels." She sighed. "You know, it's funny. If you think about it, Harry Potter flew that broom of his right up my ass. I need to find that same sort of instant billion-dollar classic, pronto—or else we'll all be waiting tables. You get what I'm saying? *Pronto.*"

Before Liz could reply, Carol Whitehead took a cell phone call from her yoga instructor and walked off.

Yes, Liz got what her mean old shriveled-up boss was saying. But she didn't understand how or why she would be affected by it. Empire had to go more literary? Fine. No problemo. Liz was *Ms.* Literary, for God's sake. She'd just read *Extremely Loud and Incredibly Close*, by Jonathan Safran Foer. (Some of it, at least.) And she loved Harry Potter. (The first four chapters of the first book, anyway.) She decided to display both on the little shelf above her desk—the hardcover editions, of course—just so that Carol Whitehead would get the picture.

Over the next few days, she added several more: *Ulysses*, *The Complete Works of Shakespeare*, and a leather-bound *Emma*. Then came all seven volumes of Proust's *Remembrance of Things Past*. The shelf began to sag under the weight.

A week later, Carol Whitehead called Liz into her office and fired her.

Liz was stunned. At first, she didn't believe it. She felt her throat tightening. She offered to work for free. The summer was only half over.

"I'm sorry, Liz," Carol Whitehead said. "I know this is awkward." The phone rang. She glanced at the caller ID. "Shit. I have to take this. Good luck with everything. If you ever want to talk, by all means, stay in touch." She picked up the phone and yelled, "Jimmy! Hi, *you!*"—then turned her back on Liz and burst out laughing.

When Liz returned to her desk, there was an e-mail waiting for her. It was from Carol Whitehead. She was giving Liz until the end of the day to clean out her cubicle. Liz had to borrow a cart from the mail room to handle all the books.

* * *

After that, Liz sank into a deep depression. She spent a lot of time in bed. She decided to start a novel, *Death of a Corporate Hag*, but was never able to get past the dedication page. (*To*

Harry Potter: Keep flying that broom of yours!) She applied for four
other jobs but didn't get a single offer—not even for sorting
mail at Columbia University. She even sank so low as to think
about trying to get back together with Damon but reconsidered
after he sent her a postcard from Cabo San Lucas.

> Hey Liz,
>   Just wanted to say hi. How's New York? I'm surfing a
> lot. I think we're better off as friends. I met Quentin
> Tarantino at a bar. The sun is spidery.
>   Love, D
>
>   PS: Your dad is right. The pot down here is unbeliev-
> able.

To make matters worse, Brit and Mercedes stopped calling.
Neither of them wanted to hang out with her very much. Not that
Liz could blame them. She wasn't exactly in the mood for their ritual Sunday "B&B" (brunch at the Stanhope, followed by Barneys
for a shopping spree)—or weekday jaunts to Sag Harbor to hang
out by Brit's pool and theorize about the penis sizes of various
celebrities. In fact, the only person who kept in regular touch over
the summer was Ned Parrish. But that was just because he'd added
her to the mass e-mail list promoting his dumb gigs.

Friends, fans, & Ned-heads! The last show was spectacular!
We nearly filled Bimbo Lounge! Come make it happen again

this coming Monday night @ 8:30 @ Sludge Fest! Only $5!
THANX SO MUCH FOR SUPPORTING ME!!!

It got so that Liz wanted to scream whenever she turned on
the computer. Ned Parrish sent her the same exclamation-
point-ridden e-mails almost every single day. It was ridiculous.
She'd alienated her friends, so now all she had was spam. She'd
been wrong about Ned Parrish. He wasn't a cool MTV2 type. He
was a pushy *salesman*. And she very seriously doubted he was
"the next Beck." Besides, how pretentious was it to claim that
you were a singer/songwriter when you weren't? It was like that
time Dad introduced himself to her guidance counselor as a
"freelance visionary." Please! Singer/songwriters got *paid* for
what they did. (So did freelance visionaries, for that matter.)
They made *livings* at it. Otherwise they weren't really
singer/songwriters. They were garbage collectors, or trust fund
millionaires, or mass-market teen editors.

For the first time in Liz's life, a disturbing thing began to
happen: she found herself having angry fantasies. She spent
many afternoons in August giggling alone as she sipped Dad's
pinot noir (he drank red wine for "health" reasons), dreaming
up ways to mess with Ned Parrish's head. She would send him
scary, stalker-type fan letters. She would show up at a gig with
a toy Casio keyboard and demand an immediate, on-site battle
of the bands. She would burn him in effigy outside one of those
crappy clubs on the Lower East Side.

In a weird way, though, she felt as if she were becoming less
"uptight." She laughed more. Her imagination grew wilder. She

talked louder, even when nobody was around. "You're an editor, Ned Parrish!" she would cry to her empty home. "YOU'RE AN EDITOR! AND THERE'S NOTHING WRONG WITH THAT!"

On the other hand, she wouldn't want to say that to his face, because she couldn't risk upsetting him. She had to get *somebody* at Empire Books to write her a college recommendation—somebody other than Carol Whitehead, who had gone so far as to send Liz a preemptive e-mail via her assistant.

> dear liz: ms. whitehead just wanted to let you know she's thinking of you, but unfortunately w/ fall sales conferences, she's too busy to write a college rec on anyone's behalf. she even had to turn down her own nephew, who's applying to harvard! she wanted you to know how terrible she feels. good luck, btw! ☺
>
> best, whitney

Unbelievable. The gall of that woman! And all because Liz's lame *Killer Rabbits* ad slogan had been better than hers. But Liz had to admit it: she'd learned something valuable about human nature. Carol Whitehead knew what it took to stay on top. If you shamed her—unintentionally or not—then you became her enemy. And she would spend the rest of her life anticipating what you wanted, denying it to you, and making you feel like shit for having ever wanted it in the first place.

Funny. She would probably get along great with Kyle.

chapter 5

". . . level may be elevated again, indicating a 'high risk of terror.' While the administration denies knowledge of any specific threat, the recent anniversary of the nine-eleven terror attacks has once again prompted officials—"

Will slammed his fist down on the snooze button.

For a fleeting instant, he felt almost normal. But then the agony started, the way it always did . . . first with the nausea, and then with that awful sensation in the back of the head (*oh God, here it comes*), the growing pressure . . . like a balloon, mechanically inflating at the top of his spine, filling his skull with hot air until his brain got mashed against the inside of his forehead in a haze of excruciating pain.

What happened last night?

He had no idea.

Well . . . there were flashes. He remembered Dad's little pile of white powder. He remembered the kid with the blue face and the yellow teeth. Rudy? No, Ricky. And how Dad had implied that he'd somehow gotten Will into Wiltshire by donating money to the Vietcong. (Or something.) And later, dancing with Brit and Mercedes but still not knowing which was which . . . and after that, wondering what it would be like to kiss Liz, then realizing, whoops! . . . No—probably better not to think those sorts of thoughts unless he wanted to go to prison, or burn in hell forever, or both.

Mostly, though, he remembered how Kyle had glared at him all night.

Shit, Will thought in a panic. *Did he somehow read my mind?*

Maybe. Twins were supposed to have weird psychic powers. And with a Wiccan Mom and satanic Dad . . . *Christ.* Anything was possible.

Will blindly ran his hand over his bedside table. Sometimes, when he was particularly wasted, he left notes for himself—cryptic, baffling treasure maps dotted with clues that hopefully would lead him (but never did) to the elusive pot of gold: a complete recollection of what had happened the previous night.

Aha!

His fingers brushed against a piece of paper torn from his notebook. He snatched it up and rolled over onto his back.

Why does Dad hate me so much?

Why won't Mom ever talk about it?

How come I never met Liz and Kyle until now?

Did I just pee on myself?

Will frowned. He tossed the page on the floor, then lifted the covers and peered down at his naked body. It seemed dry. And there was no smell—always a good sign.

He closed his eyes. No way was he going to school today. Of course he wasn't. He'd already made the decision to drop out.

The phone started ringing.

"Ugh," he croaked.

"Will!" Mom shouted. "Can you get that, honey? I just did my nails."

Will threw his arm across the side table again. His hand smashed into the clock radio and knocked it on the floor. "Shit," he whispered. He struggled to sit up straight. His burning head swam. The phone grew louder and louder, torturing him. He could *see* it, right beside his Wiltshire-issued notebook, black and smudged with fingerprints, but he couldn't grab it because his hands were shaking too much. . . . Wait, there—

"Hello?" He sounded like death.

Silence.

"Hello?" he said again. "Who's there?"

A girl sniffed.

"Who is this?"

"It . . . it's Liz."

He bolted upright. "Liz?"

"Will, I . . ." she began. Her voice broke. She was sobbing.

"What is it? What's wrong?"

She didn't answer.

Will's heart began to thump. A dizzy black dread settled over him. For a horrible moment, he wondered if he really *had* tried to kiss her. No. No way. He never would have gotten *that* drunk. And if he had, he would have remembered it.

"Dad," she choked out.

"What about him? What is it, Liz?"

"He's dead."

"He's . . . *what*?"

"Early this morning. Heart attack. He was up all night. . . ." The rest of her words were lost in a flurry of sniffling and uneven gasps.

Jesus. Will blinked several times.

There was a click.

"Who is this?" a pissed-off voice snapped.

"You mean me?" Will asked.

"Yes, you. This is Kyle Shepherd. My sister's in no condition to talk to anyone."

"But she . . . uh, she called—she called me," Will stammered. "This is Will."

Kyle didn't answer.

"I had to tell him," Liz wept.

"Great," Kyle muttered, sighing. "Just great."

"What happened?" Will asked.

"What do you think, asshole?" Kyle barked. "Dad had a heart attack. He stayed up all night drinking and smoking weed and doing coke, and his heart gave out. And now he's dead. Got it?"

Will swallowed. He realized he was shaking even more than at first. The phone bounced against his temple. "I'm sorry," he whispered.

"Sure, you are," Kyle mumbled.

"Kyle!" Liz yelled. "Shut *up*, all right?" She sniffed. "I knew you would be like this. That's why I didn't tell you—"

"That's enough," Kyle interrupted. "I think we all have to get off the phone now, okay? We have a lot to take care of."

"Okay," Will said. "I want to help. What can I do?"

"Help?" Kyle laughed harshly. "You've helped plenty. It would've helped if you never showed up at our house. Because then Dad wouldn't have gotten so fucked up, and he'd still be alive right now—"

"Stop it!" Liz shrieked.

There was another click.

"Hello?" Will said.

"I'm so sorry, Will," Liz sobbed. "Now you understand, okay? Now you understand why I didn't want to go to boarding school with him, why I never wanted anything to do with him! At all!"

Will's jaw hung slack.

"Listen, I'll talk to you later, okay?" Liz said. "It's not your fault. None of this is your fault—"

Bzzzzzzt.

"Hello?" Will breathed.

Nobody responded. The line was dead.

"Who was that, honey?"

Mom stood in the doorway. She smiled and blew on her freshly painted fingernails. They were bright red. He had no idea how long she'd been there. He tried to place the phone back on the receiver. It took him a while. He kept shuddering.

"Will? Are you okay?"

He turned to her.

She stopped smiling. "What is it?"

He opened his mouth, but the words stuck in his chest. For a second, he *saw* his mom—really, truly saw her—as if she were a stranger, a random grown-up, and everything he'd always taken for granted stood out in stark relief: the cheap "bohemian" dress, the lipstick and eyeliner, the long dyed brown hair . . . and he said to himself: *That whole getup is a costume. It's a pitiful attempt to fool everyone into thinking she's younger than forty-seven.* She clung to her youth like a life raft. Why couldn't she just give in and admit she was old and haggard? What was the big deal? Why couldn't she and Dad and Uncle Pete and all the rest of them just act their age? The drugs, the crude jokes . . . No wonder Pete crashed that car. No wonder Dad's heart exploded. Cindy What's-her-face was right.

Mom's arms dropped to her sides. She took a step forward, her forehead creased. "What happened, Will? You're scaring me."

"Dad," he breathed.

"What about him?"

"He died."

Mom blinked. "You want to run that by me again?"

"He died, Mom."

She cupped a hand over her mouth. Her eyes widened. But the gesture was strangely empty and melodramatic.

Will couldn't get it out of his head: *She looks like an actress right now.* The way she moved . . . It was so stilted. Was she reacting with shock because she was supposed to react that way? On the other hand, how could he possibly know? Did he have any idea what she was actually feeling? Grief? Regret? Relief?

In all their long, lonely years together, Mom had never told him how she'd truly felt about Dad, aside from the occasional caustic remark. ("That sounds like something your father would say, but not in a bad way.") Her body language never betrayed anything other than impatience. Will remembered the few times Dad's name had come up, mostly at birthdays. Mom had sipped her wine a little more quickly; she'd busied herself with meaningless tasks: the dishes, the garbage, the laundry . . . and inevitably the conversation shifted from Dad to something completely trivial. She'd built that Dad wall so that it wouldn't come down, and Will had never climbed it or plowed through it—nor had he ever tried. On the contrary, he'd helped build it too. And the recent cycle of booze and hangovers kept it sturdy and intact, as did his sardonic humor and his ironic detachment. . . . It would have to come down sooner or later, though. At least that was what his therapist, Dr. Brown, kept suggesting. (In a nice way, of course.) Will was just frightened of what would happen when it did.

But today would not be the day.

He held his breath, waiting for her to respond. He swallowed weakly.

"So when did it happen?" she finally asked. Her voice was calm, even.

"Sometime this morning."

"Wow." She started chewing on her wet thumbnail. The polish stained her lip. Her eyes fell to the floor. "I don't believe it."

"Neither do I," he whispered.

She glanced up at him. "When's the funeral?"

"The funeral?" The question caught him off guard. "I don't know."

"I guess this means you'll miss some more school," she said absently. She paused for a moment, then turned and left, closing the bedroom door behind her.

"I guess so." Will gazed at the bare walls. Something stirred inside him, but he quashed it before he could name it. "I didn't really think about it that way."

* * *

A few minutes later, a tinny voice blared from the floor.

". . . now here's Heather O'Rourke, with Shadow Traffic! Good morning, Heather! What's it like out there?"

Will lunged for the clock radio. He overshot it and ended up tumbling off the bed. *Ouch.* His head wound up under the side table, inches from the wall socket. He yanked out the plug. His heart was thumping again. He had to get in touch with Liz— now, without Kyle knowing it. But how? *Think!* He would send her an e-mail. No . . . an IM. Yes. Then he'd be able to get the information he needed, about Dad and about . . . his behavior last night. He staggered to his feet and slumped down at his desk. He'd bumped his elbow in the fall. It *hurt.* At least he was alive. (Was that good?) He jabbed at his computer and sat there as it whirred to life. He kept listing to the left. His head was being dragged down by invisible weights.

Come on, come on. . . .

He snatched the mouse and clicked onto the Internet.

His eyes narrowed. He had mail.

You have one new message

From: lizshepherd@webmail.com

Time: 8:07 a.m.

Subject: Dad's funeral

Hi, Will . . .

I'm so sorry about what happened this morning. . . . You have to understand that Kyle isn't himself, and neither am I. . . . Anyway, I wanted to let you know that Dad's funeral is tomorrow, in Miami. I know it's short notice, but since he's technically Jewish, he left instructions that he had to be buried within 24 hours or as close as possible.

If you can come, e-mail me back and I'll send the details.
Please come!!!

Love,

Liz

Will leaned back in his chair.

Well. That was it. He would definitely have to put an emergency call in to Dr. Brown this morning. Not only was he emotionally numb, he had just one thought—even after reading the e-mail fourteen straight times.

Dad is technically Jewish?

part II:

THE FUNERAL*

*With some additional baggage

chapter 6

By the time Kyle calculated he'd been awake for forty-eight straight hours, he decided it was best not to care about sleep. Sleep was for the weak. Sleep was for Liz, for the "grown-up"—flighty, self-righteous, and a wreck—whereas he, the true grown-up, was cool and in charge. They'd both flown more than a thousand miles. Yet *he* was the one who had conquered exhaustion. He'd fought his way through a second wind and a third wind and a fourth wind too, but it wasn't a total victory. Regrettably, he'd settled into an angry black stupor, his thoughts flitting from one unappetizing issue to the next:

a. Crazed pariah alcoholic half brother

b. Dad's impending funeral *in only three hours, holy shit*—

c. (More like c–z): Indefinable anxious concerns, flitting

the way Fat Dog flitted among the steaming meat loaf trays in the cafeteria back home . . . and Kyle knew he should be there, because Fat Dog couldn't handle prepdate.com by himself. . . . Although did thinking of Dorchester as home mean that Kyle's home *was* Dorchester? Shouldn't he be thinking about Dad? Shouldn't—?

"I don't look my best," Kyle said.

He blinked at his reflection. He was losing his mind. Only lunatics talked to themselves alone in the mirror. But technically, he wasn't alone. Liz was asleep in the bed across the room, still fully clothed—the blankets hanging off her like a collapsed circus tent, her mascara still staining her face from the long flight and the cab ride from the airport and the incessant wailing, *"WHAAAAAA!!!"*

He felt a quick pang of guilt. He wasn't being fair. Of course Liz was a wreck. Their father had just died.

Our father has just died, Kyle echoed to himself, wondering if tears would come. The lack of tears might just prove he was strong, though, strong enough not to sleep *or* cry. Liz had grown so hoarse that the sound had eventually morphed into a stuttering gasp, punctuated by hiccoughs: *"I c-c-can't believe we were down here—*(hiccough)—*a week ago. . . . He seemed s-s-so—*(hiccough)—*healthy."*

Healthy? Sorry, Liz. That might be pushing it. Dad was a drug-addled mess. On the other hand, it hadn't occurred to Kyle that Dad would drop dead so soon, either.

He chewed his chapped lips. It was seven o'clock. A beautiful fall morning in Coral Gables. The sunlight glaring through the floor-to-ceiling windows highlighted . . . a mysterious zit on his left cheek. He squinted at himself. That *was* a zit, wasn't it? Where had that come from? He never got zits. But of course he would get one today. Of course he would, because his life was now an insomniac nightmare.

Here he was, back in his old room—*just one week later, one week after Dad was alive*—in his-room-that-wasn't-his-room . . . because, really, this room had nothing to do with him. It was a hotel suite. He hadn't touched the drawers or closets since grade school. Whenever he came here, he lived out of his suitcase.

Which meant this wasn't his home, either.

Seriously, what kind of a room *was* this, anyway? The Shepherd family called it "Kyle's room," but it wasn't. He'd never taped a poster of his choosing to the white walls; he'd never added a book of his choosing to the shelves. No, in fact, it was more a *cell* than a room, decorated in slipshod fashion by Mom and Dad when he was a toddler . . . with those cheap tourist photos of Florida flamingos (*"Kids like pictures of flamingos, don't they, Forrest?"* Mom had asked. *"How the hell should I know? Let's just get this decorating over with,"* Dad had replied) . . . still lined with Dr. Seuss books and Hardy Boys novels (*Hardy Boys?*) and a cheesy Ikea desk/drawer unit and the two twin beds . . . all in that impersonal style, that McMansion-vacation-home vibe.

The comical part: Kyle had seen a dozen rooms just like this when he'd partied with his Dorchester bros at *their* vacation homes. And those bros might have had neglectful dads too—

who'd helped furnish rooms-that-weren't-rooms—but at least their dads were *alive*. Plus, none of those bros had ever been forced to organize a kick-ass Jewish funeral and shiva (if he did say so himself).

I'm hysterical.

Kyle rubbed his red-rimmed eyes. He had to stop. Hysterics were for Mom and Liz. So, on to business. If he could look at this room-that-wasn't-a-room as a hotel suite, then he could look at this trip as a business trip. What first?

Dressing, probably. Right. Go through the motions. Prepare for the burial.

Kyle began to knot his tie. It was a nice tie. Mom had given it to him for his fourteenth birthday. A Paul Smith, blue and yellow. She'd given it to him back when she could still hold an entire conversation without mentioning the word *SPIRIT*. (All caps.) Good thing Mom wasn't asleep in here too. No, the freak had taken a white pill and passed out somewhere else. Oops: another twinge of guilt. Was it bad to think of your mother as a freak? Maybe he should swallow that thought. Or should he?

No. He shouldn't. He *wouldn't*. He would shout out all his thoughts, whatever they were, straight into the Miami sunrise!

Suddenly he felt better. *That* was the key to surviving the terrible day. Shouting it all out loud! That was how he survived at Dorchester, after all: he never censored himself. He said whatever was on his mind, whenever he felt like saying it, and he not only survived at school, he *thrived*. He was the "Help-the-Heroes!" guy! The prepdate.com guy! The only bro who would tolerate Fat Dog! He was *good*!

Liz snored loudly behind him. He was half tempted to wake her up. But that would be cruel. So he shouted silently: *I will not eat them, Sam I am!!!* (Dad had always loved Dr. Seuss.) He would not swallow any thoughts or be swallowed by them. Nothing would be swallowed except for Dad. The old man might not have died in dignity, but he would be buried with dignity. Above all, this was Kyle's solemn promise. The earth would *not* swallow a drug-addled failure. The earth would swallow a rich soul (not just rich financially, but rich in experience, something Dad always harped on), and the ceremony Kyle had arranged would reflect that. He'd performed all the necessary tasks.

That was good, too. That was *really, really, really* good!

Could he cry now? Maybe. Where was this crazy guilt coming from, anyway? He'd let Mom and Liz cry. Now he was even allowing them to sleep, when they'd done *nothing*. What about him? He'd flown Dad's body here. He'd found a rabbi. (Someone named Watson Bell, which wasn't Jewish sounding— and he was also a "Unitarian Jew," whatever that meant. But still, it was *something*.) He'd secured limos and a hearse. He'd secured a grave site! (With the help of Watson Bell, so kudos to him too, but still!) He'd scoured Dad's Rolodex (Yes, Dad still had a "Rolodex") and called every single number with a Florida prefix. He'd actually gotten people to *attend* Dad's funeral! He'd arranged for a caterer to come to the house *during* the funeral and set up a spread so people could gorge themselves when it was all over! So they could feast after Dad was swallowed!

Kyle had done all of this by himself.

But maybe he needed to make one final gesture. Not for

himself, but for everyone who thought he was a selfish jerk, like Liz. People tended to be blind, especially under such depressing circumstances. So it would be best just to prove that he *was* good. He began to fling open his bureau drawers. *Yes . . .* He rifled through the ancient tighty-whities, the T-shirts he hadn't worn since he was a kid (still folded and neatly pressed, still smelling like detergent)—and soon he was throwing them across the room as Liz drooled in infantile bliss on the opposite twin bed . . . because in the recesses of his sleep-deprived mind there had dawned a notion: *I'm gonna find that button Dad gave me when I was a kid. I'm gonna wear it to the funeral to show that I'm good because I remember it. It was bright yellow and big as a tea saucer, with a smiley face on it. And when I was a stupid little brat, I thought it was so cool because I could actually stand—*

"There!" he hissed.

A glimpse of yellow. Kyle held his breath. He tossed an oversized Miami Heat jersey aside and lifted the button out of the drawer. His hands trembled.

WAR IS UNHEALTHY FOR CHILDREN

AND OTHER LIVING THINGS

Would the tears come now?

Maybe not quite yet. But as he affixed the button to his lapel in the mirror, he did see himself overflowing with tears at the funeral. He saw himself forgiving Liz and Mom for being so useless and broken during his hour of Jewish funeral need—

He saw something else in the drawer.

Oh my God.

A framed picture. Specifically, a framed portrait, a por-trait of Dad that Kyle had drawn when he was nine years old. Kyle lifted the portrait and held it before him. His fingers were clammy. *Why isn't this hanging on a wall? Why is it stuffed in my underwear drawer?* He remembered drawing it. He was nine. He'd worked hard to make it incredibly lifelike—and his teacher (Miss Miller, a chubby troglodyte) had given him an A+. *I was an artist!* But when he'd brought it home and showed Dad the grade, Dad had insisted on adding his own comments . . . on the back.

Without thinking, Kyle ripped the plastic back out of the frame and tore the drawing out of it, flipping it over to read the comments. There was Miss Miller's A+, big and forcefully drawn, with Magic Marker. And beneath that, Dad's unsteady handwriting:

This is amazing. You've got talent. But it's too *real*, kiddo. A portrait shouldn't be a photograph. That's why people invented cameras. Portrait artists who use realism are chumps, losers, straight from a how-to course—the kind of guys my ex-wife represents. A portrait should reveal the inner human being, like what Picasso did. Remember when I took you to that Picasso exhibition and I showed you the portraits of those chicks he lived with, how they all turned sour, sour, sour? And the drawings were so primitive and basic? That's what you need to go for! Your pictures should be abstract enough to get at the truth—the truth maybe nobody wants to see. Here's my self-portrait: ☹. See what I mean?

Kyle started to laugh. To think that as a kid, he'd been offended by this! To think that *this* could have made him sad! No wonder Dad had hidden it. And no wonder Kyle couldn't cry now. There was no point in getting worked up about *any* of this.

His laughter died.

There was something else in the drawer: a pile of mangled tinfoil squares that had been hidden under the portrait. They were all charred in the exact same place—as if used for smoking something . . . something other than pot. . . .

Motherfucker.

The old man didn't just *snort* coke. He was a base-head. A base-head who preferred to smoke in his son's room, no less. The squares were covered with white gook. Kyle tossed the portrait aside and lifted them toward his nose. His eyes turned to slits.

The odor he detected was . . . *carpet cleaner?* It was, wasn't it? Dad had run out of cocaine, so . . . sure: in spite of his lack of personal hygiene, he'd always managed to keep his residences spotless and his lungs full. Kyle brought it closer and took another whiff—

"Kyle?"

He jerked around. One of the squares lashed his left eye. "Ouch!"

Liz sat up in bed, yawning. "What? What is it?"

"I . . . you—you scared me," Kyle sputtered, jamming his palm over his eye socket. Damn. That really *hurt*. He blinked a few times. The dawn suddenly seemed a thousand times brighter. He rubbed his left eyeball and blinked feverishly with his right eyelid.

"What's that on your hand?" Liz asked.

Kyle glanced back into the mirror. His vision had blurred, but he could see that his left eye was bright red. His nose began to smart. And in a moment of tortured clarity, he saw what Liz saw: her own brother—*the brother who was supposed to have it together, the brother who had organized everything*—in an impeccable Paul Smith suit, clutching a bunch of cocaine encrusted tinfoil squares, with a big fat yellow peace button pinned to his lapel, at seven in the morning.

"I . . ." He gaped at her in the glass, his right eye winking uncontrollably.

Liz yawned again. "I remember that pin," she murmured. She tossed the covers aside and marched off to the bathroom, her knees creaking. "Dad got it at a reggae concert. Remember how he used to put it on and say: 'Irie cool, mon! I and I love reggae! I and I and you and we and all de personal pronouns . . .' until Mom told him to shut up. 'De personal pronouns!' Remember?"

The bathroom door slammed behind her.

Kyle grimaced in the mirror. No, he didn't remember that at all. He had no idea what Liz was talking about. She'd been a hopeless mess, unable to do anything but snore or weep—and now all at once she was waxing nostalgic about Dad's stupid jokes about grammar? About how Dad was "de mon"? Dad was not "de mon." Dad was a lousy father and a full-fledged drug addict. (And *were* personal pronouns funny?) He'd died because he'd done too much blow and/or smoked too much carpet cleaner—and now Kyle was left to pick up the pieces.

Well, *screw* him. And screw Liz. And screw Mom too. If anybody in this house was "de mon," it was Kyle. On second thought, he wasn't "de mon." He was "The *Man*." Grammatically correct. And he was deserving of some respect—even if he hadn't slept . . . even if only now he could cry, with one good eye, an anti-war button on his lapel, and Dad's drug paraphernalia in his hands.

chapter 7

Xanax was a tricky little pill. The upside was that it fueled Will's emotional numbness and detachment (though Dr. Brown would have said that this was bad, bad, bad). The downside was that Will couldn't stop smiling. His senses had been oddly sharpened too.

His suit looked so *dark*. His shiny shoes felt so *tight*. The cab door sounded so *crisp* when he closed it.

Will wasn't wearing a tie. He'd spilled beer on his tie during the flight. He was wearing an I LOVE NEW YORK T-shirt under his rumpled open-collared oxford. But hey, even better than a tie! As far as his casual attire went, he'd just assumed that Dad's funeral would be casual too. Dad probably didn't even own a tie. He would probably be buried in a tie-*dye*. And a pair of cutoffs! Ha!

What am I doing at a cemetery in Florida right now?

Uh-oh. Had he asked that out loud? Or just thought it?

Somehow he'd talked Mom into paying for him to fly down here, even though they were broke. Somehow he'd convinced her that he wanted to say goodbye to the dad he never knew— even though he'd said hello to the dad he never knew and look what had happened. Somehow he'd accomplished all this after Uncle Pete's funeral too, when Will had vowed never to attend another funeral, ever.

Then again, he'd vowed lots of things. And as the dry grass crunched under his tight shoes, he reflected on the horrendous, sordid truth: *I was secretly looking for an excuse to hang out with Liz again. And Mom gave it to me.*

But Mom must have had her own motives for sending him here. She must have been hoping that he would come back with a little piece of the enormous shitbag's estate.

Obviously, she hadn't *said* that. She hadn't even hinted at it. Mostly she'd just talked about herself, about how bad she felt for not being able to come to the funeral because Hey-SOOS was having another show and she couldn't "flake on him."

No matter. Will was here; Mom wasn't. He crossed the cemetery lawn and breathed in the tropical palm tree beauty. For a place full of dead bodies, this was really nice. Well, maybe not "nice," but peaceful. The polished tombstones were all arranged in neat little clusters, like miniature temples and monuments in a marble city built for action figures. It was a breezy blue September day. The leaves hadn't changed color yet. But maybe down here they never changed color.

"Will? Oh my God! *Will!*"

A thin specter materialized from the grave sites . . . a whir of black clothing and blond hair . . . and the next thing Will knew, Liz was squeezing him against her, sobbing into his neck. . . . *Liz! In my embrace!* He felt her tears. He felt her curls and her breath. He imagined the soft flesh above his shoulder fogging up like a car window. He wrapped himself up in the smell of her body and perfume—

"Will?"

Kyle? He tried to leap apart from Liz, but she clung to him. His smile vanished. He struggled to open his eyes, squinting in the sunlight.

"I'm surprised you're here," Kyle said.

"I am surprised as well, Kyle. . . ." Will's voice petered out. He shrugged as Liz kept crying in his arms. Kyle had been crying too—a lot, by the looks of it. One of his eyes was bright red and nearly swollen shut. Also, Will couldn't help but notice that there was something on his suit lapel: a big yellow hippie button with a smiley face.

"Have you been drinking?" Kyle asked.

Will blinked. "Huh?"

Kyle took a step forward and sniffed loudly. "You smell like beer."

Liz disengaged herself, though she kept holding Will's hand. "You do sort of smell like beer," she said.

"Yeah, here's the thing." Will fought to organize his thoughts. His speech slowed, and the next words seemed to hang like a cartoon bubble in the morning sunshine: "I had a few beers on the flight down."

"You did?" Liz and Kyle asked at the same time.

"Yeah," Will said. "Just one beer, actually. Well, less, because I spilled a lot of it. Also, I poured some Smirnoff into a plastic Sprite bottle and drank that too."

Liz grabbed one arm to steady him, her face wrinkled.

"And Za . . . Za . . . Xanax," Will continued. "See, I'm not a big fan of flying. I haven't boarded a plane in over six years. Just thinking about it freaks me out . . . because of nine-eleven. Remember? The day Osama bin Laden's Al Qaeda terror network executed phase one of their *jee-HAAD*?" (For some reason, he found himself placing an odd emphasis on the Arabic phrases. They sounded so *crisp*.) "Anyway, I raided my mom's medicine cabinet at five a.m.—and, well, here I am."

Kyle seized Will's other arm. "Keep quiet!" he whispered.

Together, Kyle and Liz began to drag Will up a slope toward a large hole. Several bloated middle-aged men in black suits stood around it. They all had scraggly hair. Their sun-roasted flesh resembled rawhide. Approaching them, Will felt like a prisoner escorted by two guards, one male and one female, the latter with the softest fingers . . . but unfortunately he couldn't seem to get a handle on the situation. Everything was too disjointed; it was unfolding too fast. Why were Liz and Kyle so angry? Actually, he didn't care about Kyle . . . but why was Liz so angry? Because she had to prop him up?

Will tried to shake free of her, determined to walk on his own. But his feeble shimmying only had the unintended effect of shaking *Kyle* free. Liz held him tighter, looping her arm around his. Kyle trotted off ahead of them.

Here they all were, in this freaking *necropolis* (*necropolis* was one of those great SAT study words that he'd learned back at S——; it meant "city of the dead"), standing among a group of men . . . four of them plus Kyle . . . all burnt out . . . like a gang of Hells Angels at a costume party . . . and Will got an anguished, prickly feeling.

These guys look exactly like the guys who were at Pete's funeral. This whole scene is too eerily familiar. Except that Mom was there, and the priest was different. The priest at Pete's funeral looked like that guy from the Grateful Dead . . . the one who wrote a book—the book Pete showed me. . . . Phil somebody.

Coincidentally, this priest looked like that *other* guy from the Grateful Dead. The famous guy, Jerry Garcia. At least, Will assumed he was the priest; he was the only one with a little black book and a little black beanie. Or was he a rabbi?

The Hells Angels guys stared at the coffin, suspended by levers above the hole in the ground.

Will wondered if they knew what was coming. *He* knew. Liz had sent a follow-up e-mail Tuesday explaining the program. At the end of the service, the levers would lower the casket into the earth. Then everyone would throw a little dirt in. They would actually start to *bury* Dad. Themselves.

According to Liz, this was a Jewish tradition. It symbolized how the community accepted that Forrest Shepherd II was truly gone.

Jewish or not, Will accepted it. Dad had died of a massive heart attack while guzzling booze and snorting cocaine. Understood. Bada bing, bada boom. Done. Burying Dad sounded like overkill—not to mention horribly depressing—but it wasn't the kind of thing that was up for discussion.

Will glanced at Cindy What's-her-face. She stood off to the side, shrouded in black, hands clasped in front of her. She looked more like a *Wizard of Oz*-Wicked Witch clone than ever. Come to think of it, she looked a lot like Mom right now, because Mom had positioned herself in the exact same way at Pete's funeral—apart from her own offspring. She should have hugged Will the entire time. He remembered thinking, how could she be so stoic and unfeeling? Pete was her *brother*. Not only that, Pete had pretty much been her sole male companion after Dad had split, aside from her lame clients.

Will wondered if Cindy had a brother like Uncle Pete. Maybe one of these Hells Angels guys. It would make perfect sense, in a sort of grotesque way. Mom had spent her childhood cursing and mothering Pete, who'd always been a screwup, and then she'd married a screwup. Mom was definitely attracted to men like her brother. And funny! Here was Will, snuggling with his half sister. And he had to admit, he was actually enjoying himself right now. So maybe this sort of genetic trait ran in the family, like blue eyes, or alcoholism, or a talent for music. And if it ran in the family long enough ("family," get it? Ha!), the Shepherd line would all end up looking like certain elf characters in the Lord of the Rings trilogy, except mentally disabled.

Dr. Brown, where are you?

"Are we all here?" Jerry Garcia asked.

"We're all here," Kyle answered.

Will blinked and shook his head, fighting to focus on the funeral. The rabbi seemed puzzled. He stroked his beard. His gray eyebrows met in the middle of his forehead, like two furry caterpillars shaking hands under his skullcap.

"What's the problem?" Kyle asked.

"Well, it's—ah . . . it's just . . ." The rabbi cleared his throat. "You see, young man, Jewish law requires a minyan at a funeral."

"A what's-it, now?" Liz asked, sniffling and squeezing Will's arm.

"A minyan. Ten people or more. It's one of the basic laws of Judaism."

Nobody spoke. Will glanced at the Hells Angels guys for a facial cue, a sign of shame or understanding. But none of them seemed to know much about Judaism either. They looked just as bored as before. Will could feel himself start to smile again. *No! Bad!* But the train of thought was chugging. Woo-woo! *If only Pete were here. . . .*

Pete would speak up. He would deliver a priceless and offensive punch line. He was the only person Will knew, aside from the actual clergy, who would ever talk freely about religion. And he would always talk about it at the most inappropriate times . . . like two Christmases ago, when they were decorating the tree at Mom's place. He'd razzed Will after a few eggnogs, pressuring Will to claim a religious denomination— because he knew that Christmas always put Will in a lousy mood, what with the phony good cheer and all.

* * *

"Come on, Will, tell me what you are! You're a Muslim, right? One of these Islamic fascists we've been hearing so much about?"

"Shut up, Pete. I told you, I'm nothing. Pass me some tinsel."

"If you're nothing, then why are you decorating this tree? You should be sitting it out, like your mother. Speaking of which . . . Julia? Hello? A little help? These bulbs don't hang themselves. They've come all the way from Hong Kong."

"Leave Mom alone, Pete. You want to know why I decorate this tree? Because it's a family tradition. That's all. I'm still nothing, though."

"Listen to yourself, Will: 'I'm nothing.' You choose to be nothing. You'd rather let the TV choose for you. But hey, that's cool. I'm the same way. On TV, everything always works out nicely and usually right after a deodorant commercial. Hallelujah!"

"Yeah, yeah, yeah . . . hallelujah. Speaking of which, you might want to start using some deodorant."

"Deodorant doesn't get rid of the stink of booze. You know that as well as I do, Will. And you're only in the eleventh grade. But that's what I love about you. You're always at your most blasphemous and disrespectful when you're in the service of Our Lord. Yet my question is, Who among ye has never smothered a dead shrub in plastic trinkets? Let he who hath not smothered the dead shrub hang the first bulb!"

"What the hell are you talking about?"

"Nothing, Will. I'm talking to your mother. Julia? Are you listening? Lay off the eggnog, woman! If you weren't as soused as I am, I'd ask you to send Will to church to brush up on the Bible! And to steal the communion wine."

"You don't have to ask her, Pete. I'll gladly volunteer."

"Bless you, my child."

"You're a sick bastard, Pete."

"And you're my inspiration, Will."

"Amen."

* * *

The rabbi cleared his throat again. "I wish I had known there would only be eight of us," he said. "I could have asked some of Forrest's friends from the synagogue and the community to come. He was a great benefactor to us this past year."

"I wouldn't worry about it too much," Kyle said. He aimed his one good eye at the casket. "He isn't in any shape to complain."

The rabbi blinked a few times. "I suppose not." He looked as if he'd just caught a whiff of spoiled milk. "But I wonder if we should wait, just to see if anyone else shows."

Kyle began to fidget.

"If we wait, you might as well dig another hole for me," one of the Hells Angels guys joked. That got a big laugh from the other two.

Will forced himself to gaze upon the coffin. He could see his warped reflection in it, leering back at him from the shiny brown wood.

"Good God, Dad," Liz murmured in the quietest whisper. She rested her head on Will's shoulder. "How on earth did they ever fit you in there?"

That was a good question. The coffin was pretty slender. Judging from what Will had seen Monday night, the enormous shitbag probably weighed close to 250 pounds.

chapter 8

"Despite the lovely weather, tradition requires that we mark today not only as a day of mourning for Forrest Shepherd the Second, but also for all those who have perished in an all-too-human pursuit of spiritual fulfillment. . . ."

Enough. Kyle couldn't listen to this garbage anymore. Watson Bell wasn't a normal rabbi. He was all hairy. And why had Dad wanted to be buried in Miami, anyway? Kyle shouldn't have lifted a goddamn finger. He should have let Liz and Mom handle the arrangements for this sham funeral. Did they somehow honestly believe that they were the only ones who were sad, confused, and bitter? He felt sick just *looking* at Mom—standing off to the side, blowing snot into a black hanky, thinking about the SPIRIT or whatever other weird crap. But at least she had some dignity.

Liz, though . . .

She insisted on clinging to *Will*. Will, the half son who wasn't even really invited, who'd showed up late, stinking of beer and wearing an I LOVE NEW YORK T-shirt . . . a living testament to disrespect and irresponsibility.

Why did you even bother coming? Kyle seethed. *You're more of a wastoid than Dad was! You're nineteen years old, and you don't have a driver's license. That says it all. Maybe you haven't heard, but being an underachieving alcoholic loser isn't really all that cool anymore. Look where it got Dad.*

In fact, standing over the casket, Kyle seemed to remember that Will almost sounded *relieved* when he'd learned that Dad had died at Kyle's party. And sure, Will and Dad were estranged or whatever, and okay, maybe Dad hated Will's mom and refused to talk about her (why, exactly, Kyle wasn't sure), and yes, Dad had refered to Will once or twice as "the Bummer" . . . but to be relieved that your own father was dead? What kind of sick bastard thought that way? What kind of sick bastard DIDN'T EVEN WEAR A TIE TO HIS FATHER'S FUNERAL?

Everyone else was wearing a tie. Even Dad's lawyer was wearing a tie. But Dad's lawyer was a whole other sack of dirty laundry. Chadwick Wharton, that old douche bag, the college buddy who'd faked his way through law school, the guy with an even bigger drug problem than Dad himself . . . There were just so many things *wrong* here, on so many levels.

"Kyle?" Liz whispered. "Are you okay?"

Kyle forced himself to take a deep breath. "Yeah. Why?"

"Your left eye is twitching. Does it hurt?"

"We'll talk when the service is over," he mumbled. He cast a quick peek at the three other old men, the bloated mourners who looked as if they too would drop dead after ten drinks and an ounce of cocaine. He didn't even know who they were. They hadn't introduced themselves. He'd made maybe thirty phone calls, sent out maybe fifty e-mails, and these dopes were the only ones who'd bothered to show.

"Kyle?" Rabbi Bell said.

"Yes?"

"This is when we're supposed to recite the Kaddish."

"What's the Kaddish, again?" Kyle asked.

"It's the mourners' prayer," Liz hissed, tugging on his jacket sleeve. "The prayer for the dead. He just *said* that."

Kyle glanced at the fat old guys again.

They regarded him sternly. Will smiled like a psychopath.

"I understand your distraction, Kyle," Rabbi Bell murmured, nodding toward the coffin. "In any case, as I just mentioned, it's a very sacred, very important prayer. But seeing as we don't have a minyan here, I would feel more comfortable if we waited. We can recite it when we begin to sit shiva. You did invite people to sit shiva, didn't you? Friends of your father's? More distant relatives?"

Kyle nodded. He wanted to shout: *Of course I did. I invited people. I made the effort. Nobody helped me! Don't I deserve some thanks? I was winging it too, because the only time Dad ever even mentioned Judaism to Liz and me was last year, after some stoned musician friend sent him an mp3 of the new* Fiddler on the Roof *cast recording, and that sent Dad off on this whole rant about Russia and the Jews and the Nazis—*

"Good," the rabbi said. "Then we may proceed." He nodded toward Mom.

Mom picked up a little shovel. So did Liz.

Kyle stared down at his feet. A shiny little shovel waited for him in the grass. He hadn't noticed it until now. He couldn't bring himself to pick it up.

He turned to Will. A shovel was waiting at his feet too.

The rabbi flicked a switch. The coffin began to descend, jerkily, into the moist brown earth. Nausea seized Kyle. This was it. The horrible moment. The Swallowing! Liz and Mom dutifully scooped dirt on top of the coffin, even though Mom worshiped Sumerian demons and Liz's religion was *brunch* at the Stanhope followed by a shopping spree at *Barneys* . . . and watching them, Kyle couldn't bring himself to fake it.

Will, however, smiled and shrugged. He bent down and began sloppily scooping huge mounds of dirt onto the coffin. Then he giggled, nearly falling into the hole.

That was it. Time to leave. Kyle needed to get rid of Will as soon as possible. And there was only one way to do that: deal with their father's estate. *Immediately.* Because it was clear Will thought this whole thing was funny. He hadn't come to bury Dad; he'd come to collect. Sitting "shiva" could wait—

Bee-bee-beep. Bee-bee-beep.

Kyle flinched. His cell phone was ringing. He fumbled for it in his suit pocket.

The coffin jerked to a stop at the bottom of the pit.

Bee-bee-beep. Bee-bee-beep.

He caught his mother's gaze for an instant. Her eyes were death rays, her lips pressed into a tight line.

Bee-bee-beep. Bee-bee-beep.

"Sorry," Kyle mumbled. His shaky fingers finally wrapped around the slender little metal shape and he yanked it out.

Fat Dog? Yes. That was Fat Dog's number, staring right back into his one good eye—but why? Fat Dog knew where he was! Kyle turned his back on Dad's coffin and clicked open the phone, then scurried down the sloping lawn toward a cluster of tombstones marked WEINER.

"Hello?" he whispered.

"Kyle?"

"Fat Dog, why the hell are you calling me? My dad—"

"There's been a development," Fat Dog interrupted.

"Excuse me?"

"There's been a development with prepdate.com and action needs to be taken. I'm sorry to do this to you now."

Kyle rubbed his burning retina. For the first time ever, Fat Dog sounded relaxed, professional, and supremely confident.

"I just thought you should know," Fat Dog added. "Call me when you can. I'm sorry about your father."

"Fat Dog—" *Click.*

Kyle felt a tap on his shoulder. He spun around.

Liz stood before him, disgusted. She struggled to prop up Will, whose head was beginning to droop. "The service is over," she said in a toneless voice. "Who was that?"

"That was Fat Dog," Kyle muttered, peering toward Dad's grave. His stomach clenched. *Oh, man.* It really *was* over. That was a mistake. He'd walked out on his own father's funeral, a funeral *he'd* arranged. But there was nothing he could do about it now. Everyone had already begun to disperse, even Chad and Watson Bell.

"And you took his call?" Liz demanded.

Kyle turned back to her. "Well, yeah, but—"

"Do you even know his *name*?" she hissed. "You're in a cemetery, burying your own father, and you still call him Fat Dog! You didn't even screen him!"

Kyle backed up a few steps. He felt sick. "I . . . jeez . . . yeah. I know his name."

"What is it?" she demanded. "What's his name?"

"It's . . . It's . . ." *Does it start with an F?*

"Hey, man," Will piped up. "Could I hitch a ride to the hotel in your limo? I'd call a cab, but I'm a little short on cash. I borrowed every last buck I could from my mom just to fly down here and stay a night at the airport Ramada. I didn't even have enough money for a round-trip ticket. I'm planning to take a bus home."

Kyle turned to him. Will's eyes were glassy. He stank of beer. And he still couldn't stop smiling. Kyle's guilt began to recede—calmly, like the tide. Who cared what Fat Dog's name was? Was Kyle to blame? Fat Dog had called *him*! And how about a little gratitude for the funeral arrangements, Liz? But that was her classic MO: side with the big fat loser, side with the drug-addled half brother, side with every hopeless outcast—

because that was *grown-up*. Kyle could have taken this moment
to point all that out . . . but the true grown-up thing to do would
be to keep his mouth shut.

So he whisked Will over to the limo and shoved him into the
front passenger seat. Then he slammed the door and stormed
over to Chadwick Wharton, who was loitering near the edge of
the cemetery lawn. "Listen, Chad, I was wondering—"

"Mr. Wharton," Chad interrupted.

Kyle almost laughed. "Excuse me?"

"I prefer Mr. Wharton," Chad said with a humorless smile.
"Classy move you pulled just there, by the way. Taking a call at
your father's funeral, I mean. I also like that button on your
jacket. It belonged to Forrest, yes?"

"Yes, Chad, it did. Anyway, seeing as my father just died,
and I've been up for two days, and I arranged this . . ." Kyle ran
out of breath. His blood pounded. He fought to be grown-up.
"Sorry. I wanted to talk to you about a few things. Can we stop
by your office right now? I mean, I know we're due at Dad's
house for the shi . . . shiv—whatever, the reception—but help
me out here." He jerked his thumb back toward his car, where
Will had already passed out, drool trickling down his chin.
"The sooner we take care of the estate, the better."

Chad nodded. "I understand the urgency."

Kyle frowned. "You do?"

"Yes. In any event, there are certain provisions that you, Liz,
your mother, and Will should be made aware of at once."

"Provisions?"

"Yes," Chad said. "And I apologize too. The service was

lovely, even if we didn't have enough people." He smiled again and then trotted off to his own car.

Kyle watched Chad go. That sounded disturbing—even more disturbing than Fat Dog's mysterious "developments." He almost yelled after Chad to ask what he meant, but the pressing matter was to get Will out of the cemetery as soon as possible—especially since Liz and Mom had wandered over to the limo and were staring in puzzlement at the drugged figure slumped in the front seat.

* * *

Once they were in motion, gliding through the Miami streets toward Chad's office, Kyle calmed a little. The words *developments* and *provisions* stopped ricocheting around his head like pinballs. He stole a few glances at Mom and Liz. They gazed silently at their laps. Will snored obliviously in the front passenger seat.

"Hey, Liz?" Kyle asked.

"Yeah?"

"Did Dad ever talk to you about Judaism?"

Liz shot an uncomfortable glance at Mom. "Not really," she said. "I mean, not except for when his friend sent him that *Fiddler on the Roof* download last year."

"That's just what I was thinking," Kyle said. He mustered a smile. "I was thinking that he got into Judaism because he loved the theater, and it sparked an interest—"

"Interest?" Mom cut in. "He only got interested in Judaism

because he wanted to piss me off about my own spiritual beliefs. Come on, you guys. This was a notion that dawned in his head when he was stoned and in a mood to cause trouble. Trust me. He was trying to play a mean joke on me."

Kyle swallowed. He wiped his good eye.

"Are you sure that's why he got into Judaism?" Liz said, her voice catching. "Because he was trying to play a mean joke on you?"

"Yes. And I'd say the funeral was the punch line, wouldn't you, Liz? I mean—"

"All right, we get it, Mom," Kyle breathed. So much for being grown-up and keeping his mouth shut. "Lay off her."

* * *

By the time the limo pulled up to the squat, glass-enclosed office building, Kyle had rubbed his injured eye halfway shut. He loosened his tie and removed his jacket. Industrial-strength air-conditioning blasted them in the lobby, a blessed relief. But while he, Liz, and Mom perspired, Will was as dry as a biblical desert—refreshed by his snooze and even able to walk under his own power. Chad ushered the four of them into the elevator, then down a hall into a private, windowless conference room. A TV and DVD player had been set up at the far end of the glossy black table.

"Would any of you like anything before we begin?" he offered.

"A double Smirnoff and soda, with lime," Will answered.

Liz laughed. She clamped a hand over her mouth. Kyle elbowed her in the gut, suppressing a smile. She swatted his arm.

"What?" Will said.

Chad's face darkened. "It's eleven thirty in the morning, Will. Then there's the small matter of your age. Something nonalcoholic?"

"A couple of lines of coke?" Will suggested.

Mom groaned and slumped over the table, burying her head in the crook of her arm, her long black hair tumbling out in an over-conditioned mess.

"What?" Will said blankly. "This is Miami. Everybody does coke in Miami. When in Rome, right?"

Chad didn't answer.

"When in Rome," Liz echoed, her laughter dying.

"Chad, can we just get started, okay?" Kyle demanded.

"Patience, my boy," Chad replied, his eyes on Will. "I have to use the facilities first." He hurried from the room.

Kyle snickered. *Patience, my boy?* That was rich. That was *too* good. And very deliberate: it was the same BS aphorism Chad had supplied on numerous occasions—the first being when Kyle caught him and Dad smoking a joint together not long after Kyle had drawn Dad's portrait. Kyle, age nine, asked if he could have a puff of weed. Dad said, "When you're older." Chad said, "Patience, my boy." Then they both laughed. And Kyle had asked himself the same question then as he did now. What was the point of being patient if you knew that there was very little in the world worth waiting for?

chapter 9

(BEFORE, AFTER, AND DUR-
ING THE SCREENING OF
DAD'S FINAL WILL AND
TESTAMENT), IN WHICH LIZ
READS A POEM AND IS
STRUCK WITH AN EPIPHANY

Liz still wasn't sure how to feel about Will. She kept vacillating between sisterly warmth and a more maternal desire to grab him, slap him, and hug him. She had a secret reason for the mood swings, too. And even though the secret was dark, she didn't want to fight it, because it drew her closer to him—closer in a scary and exhilarating way because it was something neither Kyle nor Mom could ever know. She would never tell them, either. Ever.

She'd read Will's application essay to the Wiltshire School.

Dad had given it to her the night before he died, right after Liz escorted Will into a taxi. Will hadn't even been able to open his eyes. He was staggering and slurring something like,

"You-be-full . . . be-you-full" (*did* she look full; had she eaten too many hors d'oeuvres?) and she knew right then, wistfully, that he would never remember anything about the night or the party. He wouldn't remember their dancing, their laughing, their plastic champagne cups clinking—but hey, she'd been pretty wasted herself. She'd just wanted to go to bed.

And that was when Dad had knocked and handed her a yellow envelope with a single word scribbled on it: *Will.*

"Read this," he'd said, burping and rubbing his red nostrils. "I saw you and Will hanging out. I know you dig where he's at. This will help you dig him even more. You'll read it, sweetie, won't you?"

Those were Dad's last words to me.

It was almost as if Dad had known he was going to die. Not that Liz believed in the predestination mumbo jumbo Mom did. But by the time Liz had finished reading Will's two-thousand-word-long screed—the only honest baring of his tragic, messed-up, Pandora's box of a soul he'd ever allowed, probably—Dad was already gone.

* * *

Mr. Wharton reappeared after a very long visit to the restroom. He tugged at his nose and sniffed, chomping on a piece of gum. Then he dimmed the conference room lights, spat the gum into a white-paper-only recycling basket, and sat. "Shall we begin?"

"Wait!" Liz said. "I'd like to read a poem first."

Mr. Wharton turned to Mom. "Mrs. Shepherd? Is that okay?"

Mom straightened, her face drawn. "A poem? Liz, you never told me about this."

"What are you doing?" Kyle whispered.

Liz stood, ignoring them all. "It's called 'Well, I Never!' It's named after something my guidance counselor said to Dad once. See, she asked what he did for a living, and he said he was a 'freelance visionary.' He was being sort of belligerent. And she was horrified. So she said, 'Well, I never!' So that's what this is called." Liz took a deep breath, then began in a Dr. Seuss singsong lilt (Dad had always loved Dr. Seuss):

> *"We-l-l-l . . .*
> *I never flew to Hong Kong or sunned myself in Bali*
> *I never petted zebras on an African safari*
> *I never had a threesome or made out with a stranger*
> *I never did a lot of drugs or put myself in danger*
> *I never lived like Dad, and now that he has died—*
> *I never really knew him. I want to find out why."*

Liz folded the paper and glanced around the room.

Nobody spoke. Kyle scowled. Mom shook her head. Mr. Wharton hovered above the play button on the DVD player.

Only Will seemed to approve. He smiled, his bloodshot eyes shining.

Liz sat down. She allowed herself a little grin. *Dad was right. I dig where Will is at. I dig him even more now. He gets me. He gets that I needed to make my own little contribution to the ceremony.*

For the first time since this horrific ordeal began, she relaxed. Her gaze lingered on Will. He grinned crookedly back at her from under his adorable mop of hair. Everyone else had weighed in, so why shouldn't she? Kyle had done his part: controlled the day's events, from start to finish. (Not to mention he'd answered a phone call during the funeral about his stupid dating service from someone he referred to as "Fat Dog.") And earlier this morning, Mom had blathered about how she'd wanted to incorporate "scripture from the pyramid of King Pepi into the service, since it talks about the SPIRIT."

Seriously, that was what she'd said—even though the stuff written on Egyptian pyramids was in hieroglyphics, so it couldn't have been in all caps. Fortunately, Kyle had vetoed any participation from Mom.

And here was Liz's contribution. It wasn't so bad, was it? It wasn't about taking control. It wasn't about revenge, and it didn't conflict with Judaism or even with the SPIRIT. And who was this King Pepi? Liz knew she shouldn't doubt herself or ask herself so many questions, especially not at this fragile time . . . but still, hadn't the Egyptians enslaved the Jews? But maybe that was Mom's point. Maybe she was playing a mean joke on *him*. It *was* sort of weird that Dad had chosen death as the sole occasion to celebrate his so-called Jewish heritage. Dad had abandoned any vestige of his "heritage," aside from the family money. He hated his parents. Liz and Kyle had never even *met* his parents. He'd shut them out of his life long before Liz and Kyle were born.

"Thank you for the poem, Liz," Mr. Wharton said. He flicked on the TV.

After a brief flash of static, Dad's face appeared.

He sat at a desk, framed by a plain black backdrop. He looked like a guest on *Charlie Rose*, sans the eponymous host. He wore a Mexican poncho with no undershirt. His eyes were bleary. His hair and beard were matted. He'd probably been up all night before filming this. A lone can of Budweiser sat in front of him.

"Hey, ma-a-an!" he shouted, laughing. "I'm dead!"

Liz's stomach rumbled queasily.

"Sorry," Dad continued. "Just a little icebreaker. I don't want you to be too freaked out. Even if I die tomorrow, I've had a pretty good run. And judging from what my doctor just told me about my cholesterol, dying tomorrow could be a distinct possibility! Ha! So don't be sad. Rejoice for the life I lived! I've lived through a lot of heavy shit, man. Did I ever tell you about how I swindled myself out of thirty large trying to donate money to the Vietcong? It was for socialism. For the Soviet Union! Remember that? Ha! Heh heh . . . hegh . . ." Dad started to cough. His face turned the color of the Soviet flag. All at once, he collapsed out of camera range.

Mom screamed and jumped up, running out of the room.

"Mom?" Liz twisted in her chair. "Are you . . . ?" She watched her mother vanish into the cold, glassy bosom of Mr. Wharton's office.

"Should I stop?" Mr. Wharton asked.

"No way," Kyle mumbled. "She just needs some alone time. Keep rolling."

Liz felt a tiny pinprick of rage. She said nothing. She glanced at Will. He lifted his shoulders. She held his gaze until Dad's face popped back on-screen.

"Whoa!" Dad cried. "Sorry about that. Now, if all went according to plan, my lovely wife, Kyle, Liz, and Will are sitting before me. Howdy, folks, from beyond the grave. Let's get down to business—"

Mr. Wharton pressed pause. "Kyle? Are you sure you don't want to take a moment? I can find your mother and we can all collect ourselves."

"Mom can watch this whenever she wants," Kyle grumbled, rubbing his swollen eye. His big yellow peace button glowed eerily green in the light of the paused TV screen. "Jesus, it's a *video*, Chad! Start the thing up again."

Mr. Wharton sniffed. He turned back toward the screen and pressed play.

"You first, Liz and Kyle!" Dad exclaimed, waving his flabby arms. "I love you guys, man! You're like, these . . . I don't know, these child prodigies. You're my heroes. I shit you not. I know you're going to grow up to do incredible things. Hey, for all I know, you already *have* grown up! I hope so, because that means I'll have lived a long life. But if you haven't grown up yet, don't sweat it. I'm leaving you twenty million dollars each, either to be held in trust until your twenty-first birthdays or to be given to you now if you're over twenty-one. I know you'll be responsible with the money. Way more responsible than I was, probably."

His face grew serious, in a sort of jowly, frog-like way, as he was clearly drunk. "Liz, I love you. You never took advantage of me. Just don't let anyone take advantage of *you*, okay? And listen, Kyle, I only have one request. Whatever happens, promise me you won't ever work for The Man. Do something positive with your brains and talent. Remember that time when you were little and I told you that you should be an actor? You should think about it! Because now you've got the loot to back it up."

Liz found herself weeping again. *I love you too, Dad. But how could I have possibly taken advantage of you? You were my dad! WHY DIDN'T YOU TELL ME YOUR PROBLEMS? WHAT WERE YOUR PROBLEMS? Sorry . . . momentary Kyle-like lapse. Rest in peace. Wherever your SPIRIT is, I know it's having fun. And I won't let you down. And I promise I won't let Kyle ever work for The Man either, whoever He is.*

"And now to my lovely wife," Dad said.

* * *

It was somewhere during Dad's rambling soliloquy about the theories of Kurt Gödel that Liz tuned out.

Kurt Gödel was a contemporary of Einstein's. According to Dad, he proved that time does not exist. Dad's exact words were: "Dig it, Cindy, he solved Einstein's equations by showing that the universe is *rotating*, not expanding. Space and time are all mixed up in a big, swirling soup. So, theoretically, if you get on a rocket ship and take a long enough round-trip, you can travel to any point in the past. Dig it? You don't ever die!

There's no afterlife, there's no before-life; it's all constant and coexistent, like infinite spokes on a spinning wheel! Like that Blood, Sweat and Tears song!"

Judging from a quick peek around the room, Liz figured that everybody else had tuned out too. Kyle rubbed his eye. Mr. Wharton was pretending to watch while glancing at the clock every three seconds. Will smiled back at Liz, as if he hadn't a care.

She wondered about all the different thoughts squirming in his brain. Was he thinking about his uncle or his mom? There was sadness in Will's eyes; she could see it. And then she turned to Kyle . . . *yuck*. His eyes (or the good one) were the exact opposite. Strictly surface: a flat visor, an invisible pair of sunglasses, and they concealed nothing beneath. He was probably just psyched about the inheritance, which he would no doubt use to fund prepdate.com.

That's when it hit her. The epiphany.

I'm going to write about this.

Of course! She would craft a memoir about this nightmare. It would be like Will's application essay, except longer. And the best part? She'd show it to Will and break the shell that he'd broken before in those pages. She'd read about *his* suffering and calamity; now he would read about hers. It would unite them in a way nobody could understand, least of all Kyle. Liz shifted in her seat, ashamed for being so excited under the circumstances, but Dad would get it. Of course he would. (He was dead. Duh?)

So screw being a famous editor. She would be a famous

memoirist. She would write the craziness down, word for word—just as Will had done—and she wouldn't even have to concentrate, because the words would just flow, stream of consciousness . . . and it would involve *everything*: death, drugs, her selfish twin, but most of all her degenerate/attractive half brother (maybe she'd leave out the "attractive," maybe that was a little too creepy—but then, creepy was good, wasn't it?) . . . And Liz returned Will's smile, overcome with an inexplicable exhilaration . . . She could just picture the look on Carol Whitehead's face when she sold this to a rival Empire Books publisher . . . *"But Liz! Why didn't you come to me first? I thought we had a relationship! Why did I ever fire you? It was a mistake! I'm sorry!"*

And then the Charlie Rose interview:

Charlie: *This memoir has completely redefined the genre of memoir writing. Not only that, it has also redefined the way the world thinks about dysfunctional families—pretty remarkable for somebody who's only nineteen. How did you get the idea to write it?*

Liz: *You're never going to believe this. I got it from watching my dad's televised will, right after his funeral.* (Embarrassed laughter.) *Of course, my past is a little more sordid. . . . I hate to admit it, but I also briefly interned in the mass-market young adult division of Empire Books.*

Charlie: *I know, Liz.* (Chuckling.) *Everybody saw your* Larry King *interview. And right after you returned from your father's funeral, Carol Whitehead had a breakdown, and Empire Books went under, and an editor named Ned Parrish was jailed for public nudity. It's part of your lore. That's what happens when you're famous.*

Liz: *I guess so.*

Charlie: *Was it true that you were working on a novel before this?*

Liz: *Yes. Well, two novels, actually. The first was* Death of a Corporate Hag, *which seems to be sort of a perpetual work in progress. The second is called* Backlash! *It's about a seventeen-year-old girl who is trapped inside her own head. She keeps reliving the same fantasies over and over, mostly about how she wants to establish a relationship with her half brother. She wants to break the proverbial ice with him, but she can't—because she's worried about how he'll react, because she knows he's sweet and messed up. So every time she has a new idea, she keeps thinking about him and getting freaked out because of the backlash. Get it? Like, how everybody wants to do another* Harry Potter *or* American Idol, *but not really? Because they know that if they have success, they'll be cursed for it?*

Charlie: *No. I don't get it.*

Liz: *I'm just saying that the karmic pendulum swings from one side to the other. What's in today won't be in tomorrow, but it will be the next day. See?*

Charlie: *Are you taking any medication, sweetheart?*

* * *

"Will!"

Liz snapped out of her reverie.

She peered around the conference room.

Mom was still missing. Kyle was still rubbing his eye. Mr. Wharton was still eager to leave. Will, however, was gaping in horror at the screen.

"Will!" Dad repeated from the TV. He clucked his tongue. "Hmm. All right. I know we haven't really been in touch a lot over the years. For all I know, you hate my guts. But that's cool. All I have to say is, you better have your freaking driver's license by now. I mean, come on. Enough already. You gotta conquer your fear and move beyond the Uncle Pete thing! You gotta be mobile, man! So I'm leaving you my Volvo."

Liz stiffened. *Will gets the Volvo?*

No. No, something was wrong here. She loved that car. And Dad knew it. It was an ancient orange station wagon with a JERRY BROWN '88 bumper sticker. It was tied to a specific memory as well: "This car is like your blankie, Liz," Dad once told her. "Or your favorite stuffed animal. Cindy, how come we never gave Liz more stuffed animals?" At which point Mom had told him to shut up and keep his eyes on the road.

Liz didn't understand what Dad was trying to pull. Was this some final prank from beyond the grave? He couldn't have been trying to drive a wedge between her and Will; he wanted her to *know* Will, to understand him, to get him. Didn't he?

"I'm throwing in a little something extra, too, Will," Dad

added from the TV screen. "There's two million in cash sitting in a safe in Chad's New York office. It's yours if you drive the Volvo up there to claim it within the next forty-eight hours. Chad's gonna fly up first and wait for you. We've already discussed the whole plan. Call him when you're outside his office, and he'll go downstairs and hand you the money in person. Five-forty Park Avenue, between Fifty-sixth and Fifty-seventh. His phone number is in the glove compartment. But you got to be driving the Volvo, man! He's got to *see* you behind the wheel. Otherwise, the money is going to one of my war orphans. You have forty-eight hours, starting at the conclusion of this tape." He paused. "And now, to quote Hendrix, 'If I don't see you no more in this world, I'll meet you on the next one, and don't be late.'"

Mr. Wharton leaned forward and flicked off the TV.

Liz shot a surreptitious glance at Will. She'd never felt sicker.

Will chuckled, unfazed. "Nice gag, Dad. You get that idea from *Rain Man*?"

"What's *Rain Man*?" Liz whispered.

"An eighties movie about a retard," Kyle said. "Tom Cruise was in it. So was that old guy from *Meet the Fockers*. Dustin Hoffman. He was the guy who played the retard. Tom Cruise was the brother."

"Dustin Hoffman didn't play a retard," Will said.

"Yeah, he did," Kyle said.

"No, he played an autistic savant. There's a difference."

"You should know."

"Will?" Mr. Wharton asked. "I'm tempted to ask to see your driver's license right now. It would save me the trip to New York. But I'm going to honor your father's exact wishes and give you the benefit of the doubt."

With that, Mr. Wharton left the room.

Liz could hear Mom wailing outside somewhere.

The three of them sat in silence.

This is a test, Liz thought. Her hands began to shake. She glanced between Kyle's dead eyes (or one dead and one red) and Will's live and altered ones. *Dad is testing us right now. He wants to see how we'll all deal with one final sick joke.*

"You know what, Kyle?" Will finally said. "You go on ahead. I don't think I'll go to the reception. I think I'll call a cab and go back to my hotel. I need to put an ad out in the *Miami Herald*. Here's my plan: I'm gonna see how fast I can sell that Volvo, because I probably should be heading back to New York as soon as I can. I need to get back to my mother. I need to get back to Wiltshire. I need to get back to my shrink, Dr. Brown." He drew a quivering breath and smiled, avoiding Liz's eyes. "I need help."

part III:

THE AFTERMATH*

*With some significant second-guessing

chapter 10

Kyle scrunched up his suit pants under the conference room table, wrinkling the dark fabric into clammy little folds. He actually felt *sorry* for his half brother. He never would have imagined it possible. But looking at the situation from a certain point of view, Dad had gone so far as to break down his paternal feelings toward Will in stark mathematical, businesslike terms: he loved Kyle and Liz ten times as much.

The ratio was twenty million to two million, ten to one . . . *at best*.

And then you had the X factor. You had the variable in the whole twisted equation, that fucking Volvo. Because not only had Liz obsessed about it for most of her life . . . Well, now it looked as if she were about to cry again.

"I'm sorry about all this, you guys," Will stated after an eternity of awkward silence. He ran his hands through his greasy hair. "Really. I just want to get out of here."

Liz caught Kyle's gaze.

Deal with this, she mouthed furiously, so that Will couldn't see.

Kyle coughed. *Deal with what?*

Deal with Will! Liz's lips smacked over the air-conditioning. *Deal with WILL!*

Where was this anger was coming from? This wasn't his fault! Liz sure as hell wasn't in a position to pull her surrogate-mom routine right now. Not after that "poem." But Kyle smoothed the folds of his pants. This wasn't a time for anger; it was an opportunity. Yes, one of these days he would thank Liz for that word she used, because it so perfectly and neatly encapsulated why Will was here and what he wanted: *deal*.

The whole phony persona—the I'm-too-screwed-up-to-behave-appropriately thing—it was a bad charade, aimed at getting his grubby, beer-stained paws on a sweet CEO-style cash settlement. Kyle had to admire Will's gumption, though. He'd seen this old trick dozens of times at Dorchester. Hell, he'd used it himself. Play on the weaknesses of those you wish to exploit, and then, once the guards are down, *boom!* Start exploiting. But in Will's case, the stakes were just a teeny bit too high. Kyle would not let him threaten what little was left of their family. He would not let Will take advantage of Liz's misguided sorrow and sympathy for him. Besides, maybe Dad had a reason for not loving Will. Maybe the kid was unlovable. A terrible thing to think or say, yes, but clichés like "The truth hurts" existed for a reason. Will's mother had clearly been unlovable, after all. Why else would Dad have bolted and married Mom?

So. This had to be handled delicately. Giving in to Will right now, allowing him to leave . . . No, that was out of the question. Liz would freak out. She might even bolt and chase after him. And he probably knew it. Which meant that Kyle had to keep an eye on Will, at least until this whole sordid inheritance business was finally settled.

Kyle cleared his throat. He dabbed at his wounded eye with his fingers. "I'll tell you what, Will," he said in a measured voice. "I'll make you a deal. I'll drive you up to New York myself if you let Liz keep the Volvo after Chad gives you the money. Okay?"

Liz gasped.

Will stopped playing with his hair. "What?"

"You'll get your payoff," Kyle said.

"I'll get my . . . I'm sorry?"

"I *said*, I'll drive you up to New York, you'll get your payoff, and then we can go our separate ways. As long as Liz gets to keep the Volvo."

Will blinked. "I don't get it."

"Neither do *I*," Liz croaked, as if she were about to bawl again.

"What's not to get?" Kyle asked calmly. "Will, you get two million dollars. Liz, you get the car. I get peace of mind, knowing we'll never have to see each other again."

Will shook his head. "Look, thanks, Kyle. I appreciate the

offer. But I gotta pass. Like I said, I'll sell the car and make some fast money. Think about it: What would *I* do with a car? It's actually sort of comical. And I'm honestly not worried about selling it fast. People need cars in Miami, right? Plus, I have plenty of pharmaceuticals to last me the bus ride home. If I play my cards right, I'll only be conscious when I have to pee."

Kyle scrunched his pant legs again. That wasn't the answer he wanted. "Hey, Will? I just offered you the sweetest deal of your life with no strings attached—and you're making a joke out of it? If you don't want a ride, fine. But you know . . ." He slouched back in his chair, forcing a poker face: jaw tight, gaze cold, lips flat. "Fine. Go back to your room at the Ramada and clear out the wet bar. Drink a toast to your uncle. Have fun with your 'pharmaceuticals' on the ride. You won't see a penny from us."

Will laughed.

"That's funny to you?" Kyle asked.

A tear fell from Liz's cheek. She turned away.

"No," Will murmured. "But I was just thinking that Dad was right. I probably should have gotten over Uncle Pete by now. And I *know* I should have gotten my driver's license. It's pretty amazing: Dad can mess with my head even from beyond the grave. He's always had that power over me. I only met him once in person that I can even remember, you know? Just that once at your house . . . But he still keeps ruining my life with his head games. Maybe that Gödel guy was right. Maybe time doesn't exist. Because I still feel like Dad's here, even though he's dead." He paused. "I'll tell you what. You're a businessman, Kyle. I'll make you a counteroffer. The Volvo is yours if you want it. I'll sell it to you for five grand right now. Take it or leave it."

Kyle glanced at Liz. She began to shake with silent sobs. *Oh, Jesus.* How had he let Will control this transaction? He felt a quick stab of fleeting guilt. He shoved it aside. He was doing this for *Liz.* Honestly, he just wanted what was best for the family because . . . well, none of the other family members could *deal.* Why did it always fall to him? If Liz really was so much more mature and insightful than he was, why did she never step up and take care of herself?

"I swear, I don't mean to offend you," Will added. "I'm not being sarcastic. But you don't have to go through all the trouble of chauffeuring me up the entirety of the eastern seaboard." He tried to smile. "I get the feeling that the car is special to you guys, so I'd rather just sell it to you right now. It would make things a lot easier. I mean, Dad never meant for me to get the two million in the first place, right? The whole car thing was meant as an insult. Even Dad's lawyer doesn't think I deserve it. Nobody believed I would have my license by now. I'm Uncle Pete's protégé. So why should we all suffer for it? You buy the car, and then, as you said, we all go our separate ways."

Kyle sat there for a moment. He tried to process that little monologue. He couldn't. He wanted to smash a freaking baseball bat over Will's head. How could the kid be so spineless? This was two million bucks! Dad had screwed him! But, but . . . *just calm down* . . . Will was smart. *That's* why he was dragging this out. It was all part of the charade. And if taking the moral high ground was how he upped the ante, then Kyle knew he should take the moral high ground right back. It would be the only way to prevent Liz from having a complete breakdown until they got back to New York.

"What are you thinking right now, man?" Kyle asked him. "I mean, *really*?"

"That it's a school day. And like I said, I really should get back to school."

Kyle snickered. Right. It *was* a charade. BS: the whole thing. The guy truly was a consummate actor. Like Dustin Hoffman in *Rain Man*. "Will—"

"I gotta take a leak," Will interrupted. He pushed away from the conference room table and lurched out of the room, bumping against the door frame.

Liz whirled around. "What is this act you're pulling, Kyle?" she whispered, her cheeks stained from her makeup-soaked tears.

He almost laughed. "The act *I'm* pulling?"

"This noble bargain act. You're acting right now. Why?"

"I have no idea what you're talking about, Liz," he lied.

She sniffled. "Listen to you! You don't sound like yourself. Is this about what Dad said on the tape? About you becoming an actor? Because that's what you sound like right now, you know? You sound like an actor. And I'm not pissed . . . I swear. I'm just saying. You sound like an actor."

Unbelievable! She's accusing ME *of being the actor! What about Will? He's the one. . . . He's the one. . . . He's . . .* Kyle swallowed, stung. He felt himself running out of gas. The irony was that Liz was absolutely right and she didn't even know why—for a variety of reasons, not all of which had to do with his sudden showdown with Will.

Some of them had to do with Dad.

Unbeknownst to Liz, Dad had made that actor comment in his stupid drunken video in regard to a specific incident—an incident that had occurred right after he criticized Kyle's portrait, in fact. Kyle had buried it because he'd cried long and hard before and after. Even now it was little more than faceless rapid-fire dialogue in his memory. *"Kyle, ease up, man!"* . . . *"But you hated my drawing!"* . . .*"I didn't hate it; I just think you like to be in control too much—you know, you're too real."* . . *"What do you mean, I'm too real?"* . . . *"Listen, kid, why don't you take all that need for control and focus it on something like the theater?"* . . . *"You mean, like where they show movies?"* . . . *"No, like a play. You'll see. I'm taking you and your sister to see* Cats. *How does that sound? You'll love Broadway. The actors are all unreal, but they're all in control. Dig?"*

Kyle rubbed his bad eye. He really needed to get some sleep.

Will burst back into the room. "Okay, I'm gonna split."

"No!" Liz cried. "I mean . . . wait. . . ." She locked eyes with Kyle. "See, Kyle and I planned to drive the Volvo up to New York anyway," she lied. "We want some bonding time. We plan to go sit shiva at our house for a while and then hop in the car when we're done. That's our plan. So if Kyle drives you, and you get the money, and I get the car . . . well, this way, everybody gets what they want. See?"

Will didn't answer.

Kyle stared at Liz. Amazing. Who would have thought she'd play her hand in this poker game? Maybe she really *was* becoming a grown-up.

There was just the tiniest twinkle beneath her tears. So. He'd done it. He'd dealt. The transaction was complete—even as far as Dad was concerned. Yes, Kyle had become an actor. Just like Dad wanted. By lying and by not acknowledging *Liz's* lie, he'd played the generous half-brother role to perfection. He'd lived up to Liz's impossible standards. It was weird. That split-second acting job was probably the nicest thing he'd ever done for his sister, *ever*. It was probably the nicest thing he'd done for Dad, too, at least since that portrait. Too bad Dad wasn't around to see it.

"Listen, Will, it's a great idea," Liz pleaded. "Kyle and I both need company while one of us drives and the other one sleeps. So even though you can't drive, you'll help! Plus, we can spend the time on the road getting to know each other as a family. You know? The way we always should have?" She bit her lip. "Will, you need your family now anyway. Your father and your uncle died within a year of each other."

"I guess you're right," Will said. "Wow." He smiled and clapped Kyle on the shoulder. "You know what, guys? You convinced me."

"Great!" Liz jumped up and hugged him.

God help us all, Kyle thought. His throat tightened.

"I just have one question to ask," Will said. "Any chance I can get a double Smirnoff and soda with lime before we hit the shiva?"

"You can get a drink there," Kyle said, struggling to keep his voice from trembling. "But I'll tell you what." He tore the big yellow smiley-face button from his lapel and handed it to Will. "In the meantime, you can wear this. Okay?"

Will grinned back, and suddenly he bore an uncanny resemblance to Dad. "You're on!"

chapter 11

(LATER THAT MORNING), IN WHICH WILL WISHES THAT HIS FATHER AND KURT GÖDEL WERE RIGHT ABOUT THE NATURE OF TIME

I knew it. I really was born thirty years too late.

Even though the Xanax was wearing off, Will could not shed the perma-grin. This crowd was pure Uncle Pete. He'd found the bar (Hallelujah!), and it was sweetly familiar—a lot like the bars he used to find at his mom's art openings: bow-tied bartender, bargain-brand booze. At a millionaire's funeral reception, you'd think that they'd serve top-shelf alcohol . . . but alas, life was full of disappointments. (Death too, apparently.) Still, Will had to give it up for his half brother: Kyle had organized a rocking shiva. No wonder all of Dad's aging hipster commie friends had chosen to come here in lieu of the funeral. They'd come to party. Just like Dad wanted. They'd come to rejoice for the life he'd lived!

Even better, there was a "minyan" now, so God would be happy too. (*You hear that, Pete? I've declared a denomination! I'm Jewish. At least, I'm Jewish for as long as I'm here and the bar is open.*) Yes, Pete definitely would have dug this "minyan"—that is, if he'd decided to keep in touch with the cool freaks he'd met at those Iggy and the Stooges concerts back in the seventies as opposed to abandoning everyone except Will, Will's mom, and the random broken-down drunks he met on benders.

Will drained the last of his vodka tonic. He turned back to the bar. "I think I'll have one more," he said.

The bartender, a chiseled black guy in his late twenties, stared back at him. He didn't answer.

"Is there a problem?" Will asked.

"You just got here five minutes ago," the bartender said.

"No way. Seven minutes, at least. *Ten* minutes."

"I don't want to have to cut you off," the guy said.

Will's perma-grin widened. "Neither of us wants that. What's your name?"

The bartender raised his eyebrows. "Beg your pardon?"

"Your name?"

"Will." The bartender tapped a name tag pinned to his shirt. Sure enough, there it was, in SPIRIT-like caps: WILL.

"Ha! Then you *have* to give me a drink. My name's Will too."

"It is, huh? I thought your name was WAR IS UNHEALTHY FOR

CHILDREN AND OTHER LIVING THINGS." He nodded at Will's pin. "Can I see some ID?"

"ID?" Will cried. "But I'm family!" I'm—" He broke off, detecting a rapid drop in volume and several disapproving looks, mostly from Chadwick What's-his-face. But the shame rolled right into the ether. Instead, Will was struck by the utter *weirdness* of Dad's Miami residence. It looked just the way he'd imagined it (he'd been too busy drinking to take serious note before): floor-to-ceiling windows, unkempt yet strangely antiseptic, littered with expensive art and worn paperbacks, full of contradictions . . . as if Che Guevara were squatting at the home of a plastic surgeon.

Meanwhile, Kyle made the rounds among the embarrassed guests.

"Sorry about Will's drinking and yelling . . . Hi, yes, lovely to see you too . . . thanks for coming. You know, we should probably hit the road anyway. We'd love to stay, but we need to drive to New York. Will is sort of a wreck, so we should get him out of here. Besides, there's this crazy clause in Dad's will. . . . It's a long story. . . . Anyway, we're all gonna drive together and just be with each other. . . . Boy, Dad was a kook, huh? What a joker! He definitely got the last laugh here!"

He did indeed, Will felt like adding, but resisted. *Kyle, you are masterfully fake and gracious at the same time. I salute you!*

And then there was Liz.

She, too, circulated among the burnt-out shiva crew . . . but now she was walking right toward him. And she was looking at him. And *he* was staring at her waistline, in her slinky black dress. Okay. Something was terribly wrong. Then he remembered: he hadn't touched a girl since the disastrous non-consummation of the one-night stand with Shelly Plotnick.

Right. That.

"Hey," Liz said, sidling up to him. "We're going to leave soon, I promise."

"I'm in no rush," Will said. Liz's mascara had already run so much today that it looked as if she had two black eyes: two, big, beautiful raccoon-like wounds under windswept blond—*I'm a sick pervert.* He glanced over his shoulder at the bartender. "You know, I was sort of hoping to get one last one for the road."

"Because your name is Will too?" the bartender asked flatly.

"Liz, guess what? I just found out he and I have the same name!" he explained in a loud stage whisper. "Will here is trying to deny the karma. The SPIRIT."

"Should I give this clown another drink?" the bartender asked her.

"I think you should," she replied. "Our father just died. Besides, when in Rome, right? Spirits for the SPIRIT."

Blood rushed to Will's face. *Don't do that. Don't make inside jokes. We don't know each other well enough for that yet.*

The bartender poured another round into Will's plastic cup—heavy on the vodka this time, light on the tonic.

"Thanks." Will took a deep breath and downed half of it in one fiery gulp.

"I guess it's a good thing you don't have your license," Liz remarked.

Will struggled to read her tone but couldn't. "Well, I never planned on getting . . . Well, I mean, I never . . . Hey, that reminds me! I liked the poem you read today."

"Thanks," she said. Her voice broke. She sniffed.

"No, no, no!" Will shook his head, aghast. "Don't cry!"

She laughed, her eyes moistening. "I can't help it."

"Well, here." He grabbed the cocktail napkin from under his drink and handed it to her. It was soaking wet.

"Thanks." She blew her nose into it and handed it back to him. And for no reason whatsoever, that gesture—that totally unself-conscious foolish handing of the snot-filled napkin—made him want to hug her. Very tightly. *Stop! Bad! Evil!*

"Are you all right?" she asked.

"That's a funny question," he said.

"I guess it is." She smiled and slapped his arm.

"Why are you slapping me?"

"You asked me the exact same thing the night Dad . . ." She stopped smiling.

Will furiously gulped his drink, angry with himself for violating the self-imposed ban on fledgling inside jokes. "Shouldn't we be hitting the road soon?"

"We will. Listen, I want to show you something." Liz reached into her tiny, shapely, black velvet bag. Will focused on her porcelain fingers, following them into the bag . . . the bag that matched her tiny, shapely, black velvet dress. He closed his eyes and tried to take another sip. *Shit.* His drink was empty. Time to leave. Where was the magical Kurt Gödel rocket ship when you needed it—the one that would blast him into another time via the swirling soup universe, away from his half sister?

"I found it in Dad's room the night he died, in New York," Liz went on. "I don't even think Mom knew he had it. I swiped it when I was scouring his room for drugs before the EMTs came because I didn't want him to get into any more trouble."

She pulled out a crumpled photo and handed it to Will.

He blinked at it. Pictured there were Dad and Mom. Not Cindy What's-her-face: *his* mom. They were sitting side by side in some beat-up old car and smiling happily, young and unwrinkled and unworn. . . . It must have been taken before Will was born. His hands trembled visibly. He knew Liz noticed, but he couldn't help it. Looking at this photo was like hearing a song that dredged up images of a long-lost love or catching a whiff of a hot dog that reminded him of a really fun time at an amusement park—the crucial irony being, of course, that he'd never had either a long-lost love *or* fun at an amusement park. He could only imagine. It was a unique emotion: longing and sorrow and nostalgia over a memory of something nonexistent. He shoved the picture back into Liz's hands.

"I think you should hold on to this," he said.

"Why?"

"It doesn't mean anything to me."

"It doesn't? But it's your *parents*."

"I know . . . but whatever."

"'Whatever'? That doesn't sound like you," Liz said.

"It doesn't?"

"No. You always say what you mean, even when you're out of it."

"Is that a compliment?" he asked.

Liz lowered her eyes, her cheeks flushed. *"Whatever,"* she teased. "The thing is, I found this picture with a flyer Dad got in the mail. It was for an art opening. Dad tossed the flyer, though." She pointed down at the photo. "But you can see the gallery there in the background. I think your mom must have worked there, right?"

Will swallowed. His mom hadn't exactly worked there, but he knew the gallery. It was in Soho, and it was about the size and shape of a public men's room, which apparently made it exclusive. It was also where Mom had represented that guy Ari—the one who'd betrayed her ("Everybody leaves me!"), and made her cry, and sparked Will's revenge fantasies against Dad. And now that Will thought about it, it was *also* where Mom had shown every single one of Ari's exhibitions right up until Will was ten years old . . . right up until that final tragic opening. He remembered the pre-show photo session—because on top of everything else, it was the sole opening Pete had attended, and he'd insisted on making his presence very felt.

* * *

"Why can't I be in the picture, Jules?"

"Because this is Ari's opening. It has nothing to do with you."

"But Will's in the picture, isn't he?"

"Will is my son, Pete."

"Yeah, but I'm your brother."

"Just go away! You're embarrassing me. And look at the effect you're having on Will! Look at how he's fidgeting."

"Will is a child."

"Pete, why are you doing this? Why are you ruining my night? Look at how sad Will is! Why do you think he's so unphotogenic?"

"That's a terrible thing to say, Julia. He can hear you."

"I don't care. This is my job. If you had a job, you'd understand what that means. I want to take a picture with Ari—who is my client—so I can keep a roof over Will's head! So why don't you take Will off somewhere where you two can be alone?"

* * *

"Can I just tell you a secret, Will?" Liz asked, snatching him back to the present.

Will rubbed his temples with his forefingers. "Uh . . . what?"

"I know something about you," she said.

He glanced up from the photo. "You do?"

"Yeah. I know you want to believe in something. Even if it's a lie. But that's okay. You want to believe that our dad and your uncle lived and died for a reason, right? All of us want to believe that about people like Dad . . . about people who don't seem to live for any reason at all. It's best to believe in lies. Lies are the most hopeful. I mean, look at my mother." Liz waved her hand toward Cindy, who was huddled in a corner alone, chanting silently over an unlit candle. "See?" She pecked Will on the cheek and hurried toward the stairwell. "We'll go in a minute. I just have to get my stuff together."

Will watched her disappear. *God bless that girl.*

Maybe she was right. Maybe he *did* want to believe in a lie. Maybe he wanted to believe that Kurt Gödel (whoever he was) was right about the universe (he *was* a friend of Einstein's) and that all it would take for Will to get back to the one place he'd ever felt happy (the way Dad and Mom were happy in that crumpled photo) was to board a magical super-powered rocket ship and conquer time and hang out with Uncle Pete just once more . . . just the two of them . . . and they could have a drink.

Speaking of drinks . . .

He turned toward Will-the-bartender.

Will-the-bartender refilled the cup. He didn't bother to add any tonic at all this time. Will-the-abandoned-son appreciated the gesture.

* * *

There was some uncertainty about what happened next. Will might have even napped or passed out. Time truly *was* swirling soup, at least from his warped perspective. He was aware that Kyle and Liz had packed up the Volvo and that they'd schlepped him to his hotel and then helped him check out (*Mental note: remember to ask them who paid for the room*)—

and all at once, it seemed, he was hurtling north on I-95, alone in the backseat, with Kyle at the wheel.

Hey! I'm in Dad's car with these guys! I'm actually doing this!

He rolled down the window.

The afternoon sun beat down on his face. The wind whipped through his hair. He laughed out loud. He was on his way to collect two million dollars. It was insane. He didn't even *want* the money. But hey, why fight it? Kyle wanted him to have it! *Two mi-l-l-l,* he hummed to himself, *two million in ca-a-ash. . .* improvising a little melody based on the *Star Wars* theme song. Yes, he'd found Gödel's theoretical rocket ship, and it was this Volvo. Time had indeed ceased to exist. And at the end of this journey, he would cease to exist as well. The old him, that is. Upon his return to New York, as a rich man, he would use the money wisely. He would buy back Mom's place downtown. Nah, screw that. He would buy her a *better* place. Then she'd never be depressed ever again. And neither would he. And she wouldn't have to hustle for clients like Hey-SOOS.

And Will could really, really get to know Liz. Or not.

"Okay, here's the plan," Kyle announced. He shouted to make himself heard over the roar of the nearly two-decade-old motor. "We're going to drive until about midnight, crash at some cheap motel, then hit the road again at about eight a.m. That ought to put us in New York the next night." He paused, glancing at Will in the rearview mirror. His left eye was still half swollen shut.

Will smiled back absently. The plan sounded fine to him.

He had his own immediate agenda, though, which was to approach this trip in pretty much the same way Hunter S. Thompson had approached *Fear and Loathing in Las Vegas*. Obviously, Will wouldn't be able to score any major hallucinogens, but he planned to stay as wasted as possible on booze, Xanax, and the four Wellbutrin he'd also secretly stolen from Mom's medicine cabinet—so long as he wouldn't have to do any actual *thinking*. Not until he had Dad's cash in hand, anyway. Then he planned to thank Kyle and Liz, run away, and never see either his Aryan half brother or his wicked temptress half sister ever again.

It was perfect. True, odds were about a zillion to one that none of this would work. But he'd found his sweet lie, so he'd found his faith as well. *Look at me, Pete! I can finally answer your question! I'm no longer "nothing"! I'm a believer!*

chapter 12

"You know, this is never going to work," Liz said.

Kyle sighed, drumming the steering wheel. Nice. Liz hadn't said a word since Fort Lauderdale, and this was how she chose to initiate some chitchat. How could it not work? They had nine hundred–odd miles and forty hours between them and their goal: furnishing Will with his two-million-dollar jackpot (ergo, getting him out of their lives before he could find a way to take them for any more than that) and returning the Volvo to Liz. So it was simple math. Nine hundred divided by forty was . . . well, it was definitely less than twenty-five, because twenty-five times forty was one thousand. Kyle knew this even without a calculator. Which meant that even if they drove twenty-five miles an hour the whole way, like two geriatrics (a definite possibility in this heap-of-shit car), they would still make it. Equation solved. Case closed.

"Kyle? Did you hear me?"

"Yes, I did, Liz."

"So?"

"So what?"

"So Dad said that Will had to drive *himself* to New York to collect his inheritance. Why didn't we try to get Mr. Wharton to stipulate that Dad was insane or something?" She twisted in the front passenger seat toward Will, who was snoring. "Look at him. He needs our help. He's so . . ."

"Screwed up?"

"You know this isn't right, Kyle," she snapped. "And don't give me any crap about how I'm an adult trapped in a teenager's body. We should have done something."

Kyle stared at the flat highway ahead of him. She had a point. It wasn't right. But they *were* doing something. They were giving Will a ride. Besides, if she wanted to get nitpicky, there was a *lot* that wasn't right. There was a lot that was wrong—namely, her overly intimate obsession with her half brother—but this was planet Earth, and you dealt. Will's problem? He never dealt. He could stand to be a little more like an adult trapped in a teenager's body. But Kyle wasn't going to get into a fight with her over this. And if he did . . . No, he wouldn't. At least there wasn't any traffic. Arguments were always worse in traffic. There was just . . . road. And an occasional car or truck. And a long line of palm trees on either side. *We have nine hundred miles to go HOLYSHIT—*

"Can we call Mr. Wharton about this?" Liz asked.

"There's nothing he can do!" Kyle yelled. Too much gas station coffee. Way too much. Over twenty-four ounces. Liz should have offered to drive the first shift. She'd actually *slept* in the last two days. He lowered his voice. "A legal document is a legal document, even on DVD. These were Dad's wishes. His attorney has to honor those wishes." He glanced at her with his good eye. "Besides, it beats flying back, doesn't it?" he joked lamely. "Will does hate flying. Remember? Because of Osama bin Laden?"

A smile curled on her lips, even though he knew she was trying to pout.

Bee-bee-beep. Bee-bee-beep.

"Damn it. I bet that's Fat Dog again." Kyle dug his cell phone out of his suit pants and handed it to Liz. "Will you do me a favor? Answer it and hold it up to my ear. I should keep both hands on the wheel. What with one good eye and all."

"Your eye looks better," Liz whispered, fumbling with the phone.

"Thanks. It doesn't feel better. But thanks."

Liz flipped open the mouthpiece. "Hello? Yeah . . . ? Oh, hi! Hold on a second." She jammed it against Kyle's cheek.

"Hello?" he said.

"Kyle?" the voice answered.

"Fat Dog. I knew it. What's shaking? All four cheeks and a couple of chins?"

"We need to talk."

"Yeah, that's what you said when you called at my dad's funeral."

Fat Dog hesitated. "I've been contacted by the editor in chief of *Go Girl!* magazine, a woman named Susan Kaplan. She's interested in acquiring prepdate.com."

"What?"

"She wants to buy us out, Kyle. Or rather, she wants to buy *me* out."

Kyle's bad eye twitched. "I'm sorry, bro. I'm a little out of it, what with burying my dad and all. You're gonna have to start over. Who wants to buy *what*?"

"I know I shouldn't have called you at your dad's funeral. I send my sympathies, and I apologize. He was a really cool guy."

Oh, yeah? How do you know? Aside from the night Dad died, Fat Dog had only met the old geezer once—up at Dorchester for parents' day. And Dad sure as hell hadn't been "cool." First he'd accused Fat Dog of being a narc. After that, he went on to discuss the best way to mask the smell of pot smoke (*"Exhale into a towel soaked in dish-washing liquid"*) and the reasons why Fat Dog should play the Hammond B-3 organ. Whatever that was. And he closed with a rambling lecture about how he was different from all the other Dorchester fathers because they were motivated by the dream of vicarious success and he wasn't. *"All I've heard since I've been here is 'My son is captain of the debate team. . . . My son wants to build casinos in third-world countries. . . . My son this, my son that. . . .' I don't give a crap what my son is, man! He lives his own life!"*

In short, another inspirational performance.

"Kyle? Are you there?"

"Yes, Fat Dog. I'm here."

"I know this is a tough time for you, Kyle. But I think it's only fair that you know: the party we threw Monday night generated a lot of interest in the site. Especially . . ." He didn't finish.

"Especially *what*?"

Fat Dog sighed deeply. "Especially since your father died right after. It was written up in a bunch of blogs. There were some blurbs in the society pages. We've gotten more than three thousand hits in the last forty-eight hours."

"That's wonderful news," Kyle said.

There was no answer.

"You know, you're not older than me," Kyle continued. "You piss into kids' toiletries kits. I've seen you do it. And what are the 'society pages'? Do you mean the newspapers? Can't you just say the names of the newspapers?" He tightened his grip on the wheel. "What are you trying to tell me? That my dad's death made you famous? If that's what you're trying to tell me, just come out and say it—"

"My father has initiated legal action to take over prepdate.com," Fat Dog interrupted. "To ensure that Susan Kaplan's takeover goes through. You'll be compensated. My dad is thinking of a seventy-thirty split: seventy for me and thirty for you. The same split that we had for 'Help the Heroes!'—only this time in my favor."

Kyle shot another quick glance at Liz.

"What's going on?" she whispered.

Will continued to snore loudly in the backseat. Kyle wasn't sure if he wanted to laugh or scream or punch something. Like Will.

"Your father *can't* take over prepdate.com," he said after a minute.

"Actually, my dad can," Fat Dog said. "You should have read those legal documents more carefully nine months ago, when I set the whole thing up."

"Well, then, I'll take you to court."

"I don't want to have to report you to the IRS."

Kyle laughed. "Excuse me?"

"For the funds you embezzled . . . from that thing," Fat Dog explained.

"Ohhhhhhh," Kyle said, drawing out the word. "*That's* what this is. You're trying to blackmail me on the worst day of my life. My dad croaks, and our site gets a zillion hits because of the gossip, and suddenly you're The Man. There *you* are, up at school, with all the tools of prepdate.com at your disposal—financial, legal, technical, and otherwise. . . . You've got the power. I'm proud of you, Fat Dog. I really am."

Fat Dog didn't respond. Kyle could hear his asthmatic breathing through the phone. He could almost smell the meat loaf. His foot nudged the accelerator. There was a truck ahead of him. . . . ARTEMIS PEACH COMPANY . . . HOW IS MY DRIVING? CALL 1-800 . . . The fucker wouldn't let him pass. . . . Kyle inched up toward the taillights.

"My name's not Fat Dog."

Kyle laughed again. His front bumper was probably less

than a foot away from the peach truck's mud flaps. "*That's* the best you can come up with? Your name's not Fat Dog? What is this, *Roots*? *Malcolm X*? Is this an uprising?" With a violent jerk of his arm, Kyle swerved up in front of the lazy peach truck and screeched past it and decided he *would* call 1-800-whatever to report the driver.

"Jesus, Kyle!" Liz hissed. She mashed the phone against his ear and clutched at the door handle with her free hand. "What's your problem?"

"Is that Liz?" Fat Dog asked.

"Yes, that's my sister," Kyle said. "Interestingly enough, she decided to come to our father's funeral too. Go figure."

"You know something, Kyle?" Fat Dog said, his voice shaking. "Ever since we started this whole thing, you promised me that I would get some dates. And everything else you promised came true. We got all the bros' parents to consent. We got the Hallmark testimonials. But you know what? The only reason I even agreed to set up the site was so I could *use* it. So I could finally get laid! Do I have to spell it out for you? *I set up prepdate.com so I could finally ask your sister out on a date!* 'True love is just a double click away!' Do you remember that? Do you?"

Kyle blinked.

His bad eye mysteriously went cold. Almost everything upstairs went cold: good eye and bad eye. And then, just as fast, everything went hot. The palm trees and flat highway and crystalline afternoon sky swept past him like backgrounds in a video game. All of it remained static and unchanging, too, all ahead of him—all meeting in the distance in an illusory, unreachable, fixed place: the "vanishing point," as they called it in art history.

He'd like to be there now. A vanishing point definitely sounded like a good place to be. A vanishing point where he could disappear forever.

"So let me just get this straight," Kyle said. "I'm a little slow right now. I haven't slept since Monday. You're saying you plan to sell prepdate.com to some old hag at a teen magazine—and prepdate.com was *my* idea, incidentally—and give me thirty percent of the profit. And the only way I can stop you from doing this is to allow you to get in my sister's pants. Right after our dad died. Well, here's my answer." Kyle let go of the wheel, grabbed the phone from Liz, and threw it out Will's open window.

"FUCK YOU!" he howled.

* * *

Two hours later, the car was still silent, except for the deafening roar of the engine and the soud of Will's snoring. Kyle hadn't bothered to turn on the radio. It was all religion, or country rock, or some amalgam of the two down here anyway. The sun had sunk low, lurking to the left of the highway like a gigantic prison searchlight. Both he and Liz had donned sunglasses. There was a sign ahead. PEDRO SAYS ONLY 567 MILES TO SOUTH OF THE BORDER! It featured a cartoon caricature of a goofy Mexican man: Pedro.

Kyle found the sign odd, considering that they were driving north.

Perhaps that was what prompted Liz to break the silence. Perhaps not. He was too weary and pissed off to care.

"What are you gonna do about your cell phone?" Liz asked.

"What do you mean?"

"It's gone."

"No shit."

"So?"

"Liz, I'll buy a new one." He groaned. "In the meantime, if there's an emergency, we have yours. But you know what? I don't feel like taking any calls right now. Actually, I don't feel like doing much of anything." He downshifted and switched into the right lane. "I'm pulling over at the next exit. It's your turn to drive."

Liz's lips quivered. She fiddled with her stringy hair. "I was just about to offer to drive, Kyle." She half laughed, half sniffed. "Look, is prepdate.com really that important to you? Money and ego aside, how much does it *mean* to you? Personally?"

Kyle glanced at her. His bad eye started to smart again. "I don't know. I know you're angling for a lecture here. How about I give *you* a lecture? Stop using that ill conditioner every day. It makes your hair look gross."

"I . . ." Liz shook her head. Her hands fell to her lap.

"Liz, come on. It's me. You've seen the site. We get some pretty amazing hits. And not just the true-love stuff. People are having *fun* with this. I mean . . . the great thing is that a blind date on prepdate.com is never really a blind date, because all the bros and chicks either know each other, or have heard of each other, or *something*. . . . At most, there's like two degrees of separation. So people don't take it too seriously. It's like they have this . . . this . . ." He racked his brain for the term.

"Ironic distance from each other?" Liz said.

"Exactly!" A smile curled at the edge of Kyle's lips. "But that sounds stuck-up and cynical. And everything else you think I am. Seriously, Liz: I'm not trying to be a dick right now. The site is, like, this *forum*. Where we all can talk. Or hook up. Or write in about our dates. But the most amazing thing is that it's never *mean*. Look at Fat Dog! He hasn't gotten a single date, but not *one* person has said a mean thing about his bio or his photo! Not one! And he's a big fat prick! People are mostly just funny and nice, and if they *can't* be funny and nice, they don't say anything at all. I swear."

Liz eyed him dubiously. "Kyle, not *all* of the postings are nice. I've read them. Some of them rag on their dates pretty harshly."

"Yeah, but it's never mean-spirited. You have to agree with me on that one, Liz."

"Well, say it *does* get mean-spirited," she replied with a peculiar intensity. "Or say you have a situation. Say you meet this guy and you know he's not right for you. He's handsome, and smart, and funny . . . but he's got problems. He drinks too much. Plus, there are mitigating factors. Certain members of the family might not approve. You yourself might not approve . . . you know. If there was a relationship."

Kyle's caffeine-soaked heart palpitated. He felt sick. "What are you talking about? Did you go on prepdate.com and not tell me?" he asked hopefully.

Liz grimaced. "Oh, come on. Not yet."

"So who or what are you talking about—?"

"Hey, look!" she cried. "An exit!"

Kyle eased up on the gas. Yes, there it was: salvation in the form of a green exit sign. His left eye stung. "Maybe I can find a freaking eye patch. I can be like a pirate."

"You know what I'm gonna do, Kyle?" Liz asked.

"Drive this car?"

She laughed. "No. I mean, yes. I'll drive the next shift, but I'm also gonna do something else. Two things. I'm gonna buy us a laptop with wireless Internet so I can prove to you that prepdate.com isn't as 'nice' as you say it is. And then I'm gonna go online to your dumb site and set up a date with Fat Dog. I think—"

Kyle jammed his foot on the brakes: SCREECH!

The car skidded for a moment.

There was an instant of panic, an elongated millisecond where Kyle thought, *I might accidentally murder my sister and half brother on the day my dad was buried—*

The car jerked to a stop on the shoulder of the highway, about a hundred yards shy of the exit. Kyle and Liz's seat belts both caught at the same time: *Snap!*

They were alive. Everything was quiet. Everything was fine.

Everything except for . . . Will. He kept snoring, about as heavily as Kyle and Liz were breathing. He wasn't wearing a seat belt, either. Now he was sprawled on the floorboards below the backseat. And he *still* hadn't awakened. Miraculous.

Kyle rubbed his neck and winced. So did Liz.

"You want to repeat what you just told me?" Kyle asked.

"No. I don't." She closed her eyes. Her voice quavered. "I just want to buy a laptop. Kyle, we don't need to talk about stuff. I know why you offered to drive Will up to New York. You did it for me, for a lot of different reasons—probably for reasons you won't even admit. But instead of hugging you, or crying anymore, or pretending like we're close, this is what I'm doing. I'm going on a date with Fat Dog. Okay?"

Kyle gazed at her. The sunset lit up her face. She looked like shit. He decided against mentioning it, though. He looked like shit too.

"Okay," he said gently, starting up the engine again. "That's nice. But I gotta tell you, you're lucky that I'm accepting. I've been offered a lot of crap deals recently."

part IV:

THE DETOUR

chapter 13

Will awoke to a mosquito bite.

He slapped at his neck. The air was pitch black and thick with humidity. The car windows were wide open, high above him. *I'm on the floor mats.* How had he gotten down here? He crawled back up into the backseat, yawning. His face was sweaty. His lips were pasty. His back and stomach hurt. And—*Jesus*, Liz was driving.

The car rumbled through what smelled like a swamp. This definitely wasn't I-95. It stank of rotting plant life. There was no traffic. He couldn't see a thing other than gnarled tree trunks on either side of the doors, just out of headlight range. He'd never felt more disoriented in his life—which was saying a lot, seeing as he'd blacked out more times than he cared to remember.

"What's going on?" he asked hoarsely.

Liz handed him a piece of construction paper over her shoulder. She grinned into the rearview mirror, her face a mask of excitement in the dim dashboard light.

Will strained his eyes. He could just barely discern a line at the top:

COME TO THE GATHERING OF THE NEW DEMOCRACY!!!

Beneath this cryptic invitation were illegible directions and some kind of intricate psychedelic design, drawn in what appeared to be crayon.

"I'm sorry," Will said. "I'm a little confused."

"You're not the only one," Kyle muttered.

"Aren't we supposed to be driving to New York right now?" Will asked.

"I wouldn't hold your breath," Kyle replied. "We're almost out of gas. Liz wanted to do a little sightseeing."

"I did *not*," Liz said. Her voice was cheery, almost creepily so. "Don't listen to Kyle. This isn't sightseeing. We *are* driving to New York. We're just taking a little detour. And don't worry. We have plenty of gas and plenty of time. Everything will work out."

"I'd say that's optimistic," Kyle remarked. He tapped the dashboard with his finger. "We're in trouble."

Liz shook her head. "If we were in real trouble, the emergency light would go on. You know, for the reserve tank."

"That light hasn't worked since we were kids."

"It hasn't?" Liz's smile faded. The car struck a bump. They all bounced in their seats at the same time, like three jack-in-the-boxes. "But didn't Dad have the car serviced the last time we came down—?"

"Hey, you guys?" Will interrupted. "I'm sorry, but what are we doing?"

"We got off I-95," Liz said.

"I figured that. But . . . what else are we doing?"

She met his gaze in the mirror again. "See, while you were sleeping, Kyle got really tired and he needed to take a nap. And I got sort of hungry, and also I needed to buy a laptop, so we got off the highway."

Will turned the nonsense over in his mind. "You needed to buy a laptop?"

Liz shrugged.

"Yeah," Kyle said. He twisted around in his seat and winked with his good eye.

Will peered back at him, disturbed. Kyle didn't *wink*. Some bizarre turn of events must have occurred during his blackout, but . . . what? Had the three of them somehow made the impossible transition to being a joke-around family, all nutty and close? Kyle kept smirking at him as if that were the case. The car hit another bump, not as bad this time. Will cringed, massaging his parched throat.

"Will, I've decided to embrace prepdate.com full force," Liz said in the silence, as if that would somehow explain things.

"You what?" Will asked.

"I'm going on the site."

Will's face shriveled. Now he was very, very awake. *That*, he understood. "Kyle's dating site?"

Liz gripped the wheel too tightly to respond, struggling to navigate the swamp. Kyle nodded on her behalf.

"Why?" Will demanded.

"I know it sounds weird, but I'm tired of being single," she said. "Plus, I want to write a memoir about this trip. I want to write about moving on from Dad and from being single. It's sad, and it hurts a lot, but I'm excited about it! So Kyle and I got off the highway, and we found this strip mall, which had a computer store, or more of a gadget store, really—and it was teeny, and actually really cute. . . . Well, okay, the town was fairly run-down and depressed, but the point is, everywhere, plastered on every wall and lamppost and car windshield and everything, were these signs. . . ."

The more Liz prattled on, the more Will kept thinking: *Liz doesn't sound like herself right now.* Just the way she'd accused *him* of not sounding like *him*self back at the shiva. Not that he knew exactly what her "self" was, but—well, to quote Uncle Pete, she sounded a couple beers short of a case. Maybe it was the speed of her monologue: on fast-forward, high-pitched, and pretty much unintelligible.

But mainly it was the comment about Kyle's prep school dating site. From what he remembered of Monday night (very little, admittedly), she'd railed against it. She'd *ragged* on it. She'd scoffed at those who'd joined, even her friends, Brit and Mercedes, who'd drunk the Kyle Kool-Aid and had even encouraged Will himself to post his photo. And as much as it sickened him to admit it, he didn't *want* her photo on that site.

Will glared into the darkened rearview mirror.

"The most amazing thing of all is that every sign was different," Liz continued. "Which means that they were all individually handmade. And there were hundreds of them." Liz smiled at him as she drove, uttering these last three words as if she were unlocking some great cosmic mystery—as terrifying and profound as Gödel's theory of time itself. "So I just had to check out what all the fuss was about. The guy at the computer store said there would be 'some crazy shit going down.'"

In spite of his better instincts, Will turned to Kyle, tapping him on the shoulder for clarification. "Is this true?"

"Yeah," Kyle said.

"Including the prepdate.com stuff?"

"Yeah," Kyle repeated, a little more forcefully. "Is that a problem?"

"No! I mean, no—it's just . . . Why are we doing this?" Will tried once more.

"Because I'm all about the 'crazy shit' now," Kyle said, forcing a grim laugh. "As long as this Gathering of the New Democracy has food. Edible food, I mean. The problem is, I don't think a party thrown by hicks in the middle of nowhere will be catered." He turned and looked at Will. "What do you think?"

* * *

Several minutes later, they emerged in a wide, weed-choked field.

At the far end stood a crumbling factory, surrounded by cars and flatbed pickup trucks, all rusted and all parked haphazardly,as if they'd arrived at the site of a demolition derby. The factory's broken windows pulsated with bass and drums, muffled laughter, and different-colored lights, some of which seemed to emanate from indoor bonfires. There was a lone smokestack, too. It was painted to resemble a giant penis. Or at least it seemed to be. The Volvo's headlights had died, so it was too dark to get a clear look.

"We're here!" Liz shouted.

"Maybe I was wrong," Kyle joked. "Maybe it *will* be catered."

The car rolled to a stop. The engine made a disturbing sputter, like it was choking on the last drops of gas in the tank. Not that Will knew cars.

Liz unsnapped her seat belt and turned toward him. A few lone strands of blond hair hung in her moonlit face, turning her (from his baffled eyes) into a supernatural being out of a children's story—a tree nymph, a good witch. "So, are you psyched?"

Will hadn't the slightest clue how to answer that.

"Well, I might be going out on a limb here, but I bet Will is curious as to exactly how this little pit stop fits into your memoir," Kyle said. "Frankly, I'm curious myself."

"How could I *know* that until we go in there, you guys? Duh! That's the whole point. We just can't pass it up. We're *here*. It's part of the adventure. A road trip with a random pit stop always makes for good reading. We've gotta go in there and do this."

"I think I'm just gonna stay put," Kyle said. "I don't want anybody here to mess with the car. I don't really want to be featured much in your memoir, anyway."

Liz laughed. "Nobody will mess with the car."

Kyle laughed back. The sound of it reminded Will of a Doberman's bark. "You're right, Liz! Nobody in a godforsaken wasteland would mess with a stranger's car! Why would they? It's a party, ma-a-a-n! A celebration of peace and love, d-u-u-u-de!"

"I'll only be a minute, okay?" Liz said, as if she hadn't heard him. "And I'll definitely bring back some food for you. Will? What do you say? You want to come in for a second? We won't be long, I promise."

Will hesitated, glancing between the two of them. "I just think I need to wake up a little more. You go on ahead. I'll find you."

"Well, okay, but don't dillydally." She caught his gaze, her smile widening. Then she leapt out of the car and slammed the door behind her.

Will stared at her as she disappeared into the shadows. He couldn't stop himself from following the shapely curve of her back down to her butt. He hung his head. "So Liz is tired of being single, huh?" he muttered.

"That's right," Kyle replied. "She wants to go out with my friend Fat Dog. You met him the night you decided to show up in our lives. Remember?"

"Yeah, I think so. But Kyle . . ." Will sagged into the upholstery.

"What?"

"Never mind."

"Don't 'never mind' me. I'm too tired for it, and the only reason I'm doing this is so you can get your two million and then get out of our lives forever." Kyle turned in the front seat and stared at Will, his perfectly chiseled face carved in a look of such monumental sourness, it deserved to be preserved in stone and hung in a museum. "So what were you going to say?"

"I was going to say you're an even bigger prick than that smokestack out there."

"Right back at you, bro."

"I was also gonna say that your eye looks better. You're a handsome guy, Kyle."

Kyle shifted back in his seat, facing forward. "Thanks. Why are you such an asshole, Will?"

"Because I don't allow myself to feel things," Will replied, absently glancing around the makeshift parking lot. He sniffed his armpits under his rumpled blazer, with one eye on the rearview mirror—hoping Kyle wouldn't notice, which Kyle did, of course. *Jeez.* He really needed to shower sometime soon. "That's what my shrink, Dr. Brown, says anyway," Will finished, straightening. "It's also what my mom says. She doesn't say it in as nice a way, though. How about you, Kyle? Why are *you* such an asshole?"

"I'm not."

"Right." Will sighed. "So look, now that we've taken our brotherhood to the next level, let me ask you a question: If Liz wants to go out with your friend Fat Dog . . . Wait, I'm sorry. Let me back up a second. I may be wrong, but he's your assistant, right? The one who looks like he's ten years old?"

A smile spread across Kyle's face. "That's the one."

"So why does she need prepdate.com? Why can't you just give her his number?"

"See for yourself," Kyle said. "She wants *him* to find *her*." He reached down under his seat and pulled out a nylon computer case. The price tag still dangled from the handle. He unzipped it with a dramatic flourish and flipped open the screen, cuing the catchy little Microsoft Windows theme: *Ding-dong-ding-DING*.

After pecking at the keys for a few seconds, Kyle gingerly handed over the laptop. It still had that store-bought smell, that dust-free look of all brand-brand-new appliances. And as Will placed it on the seat beside him, in the middle of this god-forsaken wasteland, he couldn't help but feel as if he were celebrating Christmas in hell.

Kyle was Satan (or Santa? Or both? *Satan* was an anagram of *Santa*, after all) because the gift he gave confirmed Will's worst fears: it was that same photo Liz had sent him after they'd spoken on the phone—the black-sweater imposter Gwyneth Paltrow photo. Only this time, the last of her vital stats had changed:

Name: Liz Shepherd
Age: 17
Weight: None of your business!
School: Wiltshire
Interests: Finding a great big man with a great big heart!!!

"She's tired of the bros at her school, Will," Kyle said in the silence. "And she's always had a secret crush on Fat Dog."

"Does Liz call him Fat Dog too?"

Kyle snickered. "He likes being called Fat Dog. What? You don't believe me?"

"I don't know what to believe. I just woke up. Everything seems a little weird right now. I mean, I thought you guys hated each other."

"Who? Me and Fat Dog?"

"No, you and Liz."

Kyle whirled around in his seat again. "Liz is my *sister*, Will," he snapped.

"Yeah, I get that."

"Do you?"

"No. Actually, I don't. I can't figure it out between you." Will closed his bleary eyes for a moment. "Explain it to me. Really, Kyle, I'm not trying to be a dick. I just want to know why you both seem so happy about how Liz wants to go out with this big fat loser. I don't believe she has a crush on him. Something else is going on. What is it?"

Kyle faced forward. "None of your business."

Right. Pestering Kyle would get him nowhere. So, had he been wrong about Liz? Maybe he'd built her up in his mind. Maybe he'd wanted her to be that wicked temptress—wicked with attention and sympathy solely for *him*. He just couldn't believe that she would go out with that guy unless—maybe she acted ditzy because she *was* a ditz? Maybe she acted flirty because she *was* a flirt? But no, she was smart, and she was per- fect looking . . . In a lot of ways, she was pretty much everything her twin brother was too. Maybe the old superstition was false:

maybe there wasn't a "good" twin or an "evil" twin. Maybe all twins were evil. They did have weird psychic powers, after all.

"Thinking about Liz, huh, Will?" Kyle asked.

"I am." Will closed the laptop and handed it to Kyle.

Kyle zipped the computer back in its case. "I'm gonna get some more shut-eye," he said. "Would you mind hanging out? It would be a help. I want the car guarded. I don't want anything stolen by drugged-out delinquents." He shoved the case under his feet, then grabbed the recliner and flipped it, slamming his seat into Will's knee.

"Ouch!"

"Sorry," Kyle said.

Will turned toward the factory. The music blared. It was hypnotic and repetitive (and yes, he hated techno), but it *was* drug music, the music you forget to. The lights flashed. The laughing voices beckoned. He couldn't sit still. Energy coursed through him. He was awake now. No way was he staying in this car.

Which meant—

He had two choices.

One: He could get fucked up again. He could *stay* fucked up until New York. He could pretend Uncle Pete was by his side. The drugs he would need to help him along in this fantasy would be inside. . . . There would definitely at least be Ecstasy. Please, at a party like this? Ecstasy would make the remainder of his journey tolerable. It would conjure Pete's SPIRIT from the dead. It would allow them to rage together, like they always should have, if only for a few hours—and then he would pass out.

Two: He could go in there and find Liz and demand to know the truth about this Fat Dog situation and what had happened while he was asleep.

Either way, he was leaving.

"You think Liz will really come right back?" he asked.

"Patience, my boy," Kyle replied, yawning.

Will threw open the back door and bolted.

"Will, hey!" Kyle shouted. "What are you doing? Stick around! I need a guard!"

But Will was already gone. He didn't even bother to shut the door behind him.

chapter 14

**(AFTERWARD), IN WHICH
KYLE TRIES TO ANALYZE HIS
BEHAVIOR AND MOTIVES IN
REGARD TO HIS FAMILY AND
ALSO FAINTS FOR THE FIRST
TIME**

Kyle watched Will scamper across the field toward the condemned factory. This whole entire scene was something out of a Stephen King novel. *Children of the Corn* meets *The Shining*? But set on a KKK compound. Should Kyle join the chase? Maybe. He was hot. He was hungry, too. There might be food in there. Insects buzzed around him. Freaking mosquitoes. And the stink of this field . . . What kind of animals shat here? Raccoons? Mules? Cows? Humans?

Or maybe he shouldn't join the chase. He could very easily get back on the highway and drive to New York himself. He could ditch Will *and* Liz. (If they weren't out of gas. No, there was probably enough to get him to the nearest gas station. They'd passed one back in town.) And if Liz wanted to go to this heinous party so badly, she should be allowed to stay for its duration.

Kyle would square it with Fat Dog; he would forward Liz's recently updated bio; he would have Fat Dog call her on her cell phone. All would be well. As for Will . . .

He could find his own way home. Kyle didn't owe Will squat. He only owed Liz. Which meant of course that he *couldn't* leave. She'd done a nice thing with this Fat Dog deal—*more* than a nice thing. But that was what pissed him off; that was what *always* pissed him off: Liz's niceness. The "nice" way she flip-flopped between the uptight maternal adult and the clueless, dumb-ass hot chick. And the way people found that charming. Specifically, Dad and Will and Fat Dog.

"I thought you guys hated each other."

Kyle couldn't get that damn comment out of his head, even though Will had tossed it off without a thought, just like every other glib, asinine thing he said. How could Kyle hate his own sister? Will didn't even *know* Kyle. He sure as hell didn't know Liz. He thought he did, but he didn't. The Liz on this car ride wasn't the *real* Liz. Kyle himself had glimpsed the real Liz only twice in the last few days: first, when she'd called Will on her own the morning Dad died, and second, when he'd nearly killed them both back on the highway. Those were the only times she'd finally let her guard down.

Besides, Kyle had engineered this stupid trip solely to keep an eye on Will so that Will wouldn't pull any moves about their dad's money and mostly so that Liz wouldn't fret over him, post-funeral. Kyle had endured enough of Liz's fretting.

Unfortunately, the plan seemed to backfiring now that both of them were gone. . . .

Kyle jiggled the car keys. He glanced toward the factory. Part of him couldn't help but revel in the schadenfreude (a killer SAT vocab word): "a malicious satisfaction in the misfortunes of others." Will was bent on finding out why Liz wanted to hook up with Fat Dog—and Kyle knew that Liz would never tell him. No, telling Will would mean admitting that she was trying to help out her own twin brother. And she would never do that, for reasons as obvious as that giant penis smokestack in the moonlight: *Liz doesn't like me. She's just bound to me because we're family.*

But screw it. Why *would* she like him? He was vindictive, cruel, et cetera (place all of her adjectives here). Even Dad had accused him of being "not a nice person." He wondered if Dad had ever accused Will of the same thing. Probably not. He hardly ever spoke to Will. He hardy ever spoke *about* Will— except for a few times, when Mom had screamed at him for not getting over his first wife. It was always something painful and predictable too, along the lines of *"This isn't about Will, Forrest! This is about Julia! You only talk about Will when she comes up! You still have feelings for her! So fine! Go pay her a visit! Go give her a screw for old times' sake!"*

After which Dad had always just stalked off and gotten high.

Not that this had to do with the business at hand. Dad might not have wanted to bond with Will, but Will sure as hell seemed intent on bonding with Dad's daughter. (Weirdly so.) And he shouldn't be; he should be prostrating himself in sorrow before God, the SPIRIT, and whoever else—or at the very least, he should be out here learning how to drive. It was a perfect place for a lesson, too—a big, open field. Chad would want to see a demonstration before he handed over the two million. He was very thorough in spite of his various addictions, not to mention fiercely loyal to Dad. Best-case scenario: Chad would be content with watching Will drive around the block outside his law offices—

"What are you doin' out here?" a goofy female voice asked. "The fun's inside!"

Kyle flinched. A skinny African American girl was poking her head in through the open window. She wore a plain blue T-shirt with a huge logo: WHITE TRASH AND PROWD OF IT!!! She wasn't alone. Somehow, during Kyle's internal rant, a dozen other kids had stealthily surrounded the car. All were wearing overalls. Several of their faces were covered with what looked like war paint. Many were missing teeth. Kyle began to panic. The back door was still open. *Will, you asshole . . .* This wasn't *Children of the Corn* meets *The Shining*; it was *Lord of the Flies* meets *Deliverance.* Or Jonestown? Or the Manson family? He struggled to start the car, but his hands were too shaky.

"Don't be scared, darling," the girl murmured.

"What *is* this place, anyway?" he asked, finally giving up on trying to shove the key in the ignition.

"It's whatever you want it to be."

Nice. Can it be Chadwick Wharton's office in New York? Or how about Fat Dog's room at Dorchester? How about anywhere but here?

The girl opened the passenger door and extended a hand. "This is your first gathering, right? Your friends are getting it."

"What do you mean, my friends?"

"Your two friends who just ran inside!"

He frowned, relaxing slightly. "You've seen them?"

"We see *everything*, sweetheart!" the girl cried. "Anyway, I know who that girl is! She's Liz Shepherd from prepdate.com! True love is just a double click . . ."

Her voice faded to blackness and silence.

* * *

Kyle had never fainted before. He couldn't have been out for long. Maybe only a few seconds, even. He was still slumped in the passenger seat; it was still night. The skinny African American girl was still standing right beside him. But he felt as if he'd just gotten up from a nap he hadn't wanted to take. His heart fluttered. His breathing was shallow. He really needed to start taking care of himself again.

"Are you a narcoleptic?" she asked.

He shook his head. "Um, no. Not that I know of."

"Honey pie, come with me. You don't look so good."

"Wait. How do you know about prep . . . ?" He didn't finish.

"About prepdate.com, you mean?" she said in a teasing

voice. "What? You think that just because we're from Georgia we don't know what the Internet is?"

"Is that where we are?"

"Yeah. Well, close. We're sort of on the border. It's kinda no-man's-land. Come on! You passed out just now. You look like you could use some water."

Kyle blinked and rubbed his bad eye—then froze. The crowd had mysteriously vanished. He and this girl were all alone. Crickets chirped in his ear; bugs buzzed around him. Shit. Maybe he *had* been out for a long time.

"Are you sure you're okay?" she asked, kneeling beside the car. "Look, sweetie, come with me. You should meet Robby. He owns this place. He won't bite."

Kyle hesitated.

"What's the matter?" she asked.

"I think you're insane," Kyle said. "Or I am. Or you're a genie."

"Well, isn't that just like a man!" she exclaimed.

"And *how* do you know about prepdate.com? I mean, sorry to keep asking about this . . . but you recognized Liz. . . ."

"Robby found the site," she said. "Robby finds everything. He found this place for us. It used to be this pillow factory, but then it was a meth lab. And he cleaned it up."

"I . . . it . . . what—who's Robby?"

The girl took his hand again. "That's what I want you to find out!"

Kyle resisted her tug at first, but finally he acquiesced. He stumbled out of the car. His head spun in the sticky southern air. He tried to smile, just for manners' sake. He had trouble gaining his footing. The grass was soft and uneven.

"Are you on something?" the girl asked.

"No!" Kyle barked, a little too loudly.

The girl pulled her hand away. "Well, pardon *meee*," she drawled. "I didn't mean to offend."

"No. I'm sorry." The sky and Volvo and field and factory whirled before him. He swayed, fighting to stay balanced. "I don't mean to be rude, and I'm not on something. I just want to know: how did this Robby dude find out about prepdate.com?"

"He finds *all* the sites that promote the New Democracy. That's just what he does. Now are you gonna come with me or not?"

"Sites that promote the New Democracy," Kyle repeated.

"Yeah. Sites that knowingly or unknowingly create a coalition, and sites that don't judge what we do or say. Like, you know how we think about sex all the time? Or how we cry when a kitten dies but not when a guy's face gets blown off? Or how we make ourselves throw up in all sorts of ways? He wants us to talk about that." She grinned sheepishly and wriggled her eyebrows. "And listen here—*I* was the one who recognized Liz Shepherd. She is so fiiine! I'm gonna get me some of that."

Kyle's knees buckled. The girl rushed forward and grabbed him. "Honey pie, you really should hydrate. I don't want you to pass out again."

Neither do I. No, mostly he wanted to find Liz and get back on the road. And with any luck, they could leave Will here—it seemed like his kind of place. And then he could find out why the hell Liz was so obsessed with Will anyway.

"Lead the way," he breathed.

"Okeydokey, then!"

She threw her hip against his. He threw his arm around her. He resisted the temptation to lean in and kiss her on the cheek. He was proud of that.

chapter 15

The whirlwind began the moment Liz opened the front door. Or rather, it began when she moved the door aside. It wasn't attached at the hinges; it was propped precariously against the rotted door frame. But everybody else moved the door aside and propped it up again, so that's what she did too. When in Rome . . .

(THAT NIGHT), IN WHICH LIZ EXPERIENCES AN EPIPHANY, COMPOSES A LETTER IN HER HEAD TO BRIT AND MERCEDES, AND AGREES TO INGEST A MYSTERIOUS WHITE PILL

She'd walked into *Fight Club*.

Normally, she hated making mental movie comparisons because that was a Kyle thing to do. And the truth was, she hadn't thought about *Fight Club* since she'd seen it, last spring, on a Friday night, with Brit and Mercedes and Damon over at Damon's place. Damon had gotten stoned and fallen asleep within the first twenty minutes (big surprise), but Liz and Brit and Mercedes were riveted, and not just because of Brad Pitt. The house where Brad Pitt lived was just like this one: a monstrous heap of splintered wood and chipped paint, stocked with grim Salvation Army furniture, pockmarked with leaks and holes. . . . But somehow, it wasn't depressing— because Brad Pitt wasn't a homeless squatter (well, he was, but by choice), so there was *symbolism*. He was a revolutionary, and there was a *design* in his decrepitude, a secret plan.

There was a plan here as well. She knew it. The trick was to find out what. The trick was to forget about Brit and Mercedes, even though she felt a pang for them, and Fat Dog (God, what *was* his name?), and Kyle, and even Dad. The trick was to forget everything and everyone except Will and maybe even discover something new.

Had Will followed her in here?

A couple of kids in the front hall smiled at her. They all wore black turtlenecks, even though the temperature was probably somewhere in the mid-nineties. Their faces and shirts were bathed in sweat.

"Howdy," one of them said.

Liz tried to smile back. Her nose wrinkled. She caught a whiff of something foul. "What's that smell?"

"Meth," they answered in unison, and then laughed.

"What?"

"Crystal. It's hard to get rid of the odor. Listen, I'm sorry, but can I ask you something? Are you Liz Shepherd from prepdate.com?"

Am I . . . ?

The hallway spun. Liz fought to catch her breath, yet the dizziness was strangely intoxicating. She knew there had to be a rational explanation, but she'd rather not hear it or even figure it out. A connection had blossomed out of nowhere, and that was fine for now—because maybe Mom's occult mumbo jumbo wasn't hooey after all. . . . Maybe what you can't see *is* real, and it can only be chalked up to fate or the SPIRIT. No, right now, Liz wanted only one thing: to tell Brit and Mercedes, and Will, that somewhere in the middle of nowhere, four beefy strangers in black turtlenecks knew who she was. She was famous. It was a *sign*. So . . . the trick *wasn't* to forget. How could it be?

"I am Liz Shepherd of prepdate.com," she replied, once she was able to get a grip.

"I knew it," the guy said. He turned and winked at his friends. "She likes turning on and getting turned on. And reading. And dreaming."

"And connecting," she added, and they all laughed again.

They were big and sweaty and they were leering at her, but she felt no fear. She even managed to forget about Will for a moment. She put imaginary pen to paper.

* * *

Dear Brit and Mercedes,

I wish you guys were here! You would so love this place. Remember when we saw Fight Club? *It's like that. I mean, it's falling apart and unsanitary, and I can't find a bathroom, but there are so many people. The coolest part is that there's no main space, not even a dance floor. It's just dozens and dozens of rooms along these long industrial halls, and you just float around and do whatever you want. There's tattooing in one (real tattooing with a buzzing needle!), and in another I saw these girls who were blowing bubbles and face painting, and they asked if I wanted to make out with them (I've never been tempted to switch-hit; have you guys?), and upstairs there's a karaoke machine, although it's hard to get to it because the stairs aren't safe.*

The guy who owns this place is named Robby. He's nineteen and sort of cute in a burly, ex-convict way. He's bald and has a scar on his skull but the sweetest smile. He reminds me of Will, because he's alone in the world. His parents died in an accident—faulty SUV air bags—so he got millions of dollars. He told me about how he used to be in a crappy gang. They all used to camp out at this factory and use it as a meth lab. Some of them still do, but Robby doesn't like that because the smell is really awful and it can attract cops. But he lets them do what they want. When Robby's parents died, instead of split- ting town, he decided to take care of the gang and even the rival gang—all his friends and enemies—if they agreed to one thing: NO MORE CRAP.

And they agreed.

Can you imagine that? Can you imagine if Kyle agreed to NO MORE CRAP? Or better yet, if Kyle and I had met

Will under entirely different circumstances? Imagine if we'd met him here. Or on prepdate.com . . . Oh, hey—which reminds me! They all know about prepdate.com down here! And Robby knows who you guys are too! He rattled off your vital stats. "Brit: B&B (brunch and Barneys). Mercedes: geek chic." See, he and his friends spend all day on the Internet, and they troll for sites that have a good vibe, and sometimes they even get in touch with people. Have you noticed a few weird-looking southern guys and girls on the site? That's where they come from.

There's only one rule here: No fighting. (So it's not really like Fight Club.*) Robby says the trick is "never asking somebody what they believe in. It's more fun to ask what they* don't *believe in. Believing in something is crap." The weird thing is, I said almost the exact same thing to Will! You guys . . . Okay. I know this all sounds incredibly hokey and made-up, like some kind of fantasy based on* The Electric Kool-Aid Acid Test, *but if you were here, you'd see it's for real.*

Anyway, I see Will! I gotta go! Miss you guys!

xoxoxoxo—

Liz

* * *

"Hey, Liz!" Will called.

He ran toward her down the hall, his lungs heaving. His face glistened with sweat. He looked as if he'd gone for a sauna in formal wear . . . which was sort of cute in a dark, doomed-to-leave-a-beautiful-corpse way, what with his rumpled dark suit and an open-collared shirt. Dad's big yellow smiley face pin hung crookedly from his lapel.

"Hey, yourself," she said.

"I've been looking for you. I got a surprise for you." He grinned mischievously and reached into his suit jacket pocket, then opened his fist.

Two white pills stared back at her from his shaky palm, two blank eyes.

"What's that?" she asked.

"It's E," he said. "So what do you think?"

Liz's breath quickened. "I've never done E before. What's it like? I mean, I've been around people who are on it." She tried to smile. "Dad, for one."

"It's fun," Will promised. "And it's safe. Way safer than coke." He brushed his damp bangs out of his eyes and leaned in close. "Trust me. It doesn't last long. Five hours, tops. We have time, right? We'll take it and then go find some food for Kyle, and then we'll be back in here just as it kicks in. Anyway, it's his turn to drive."

She fidgeted in her heels, suddenly very self-conscious of how overdressed she was—and dressed for a funeral, no less: all in black. "Where did you get it?"

"This girl sold it to me." He wiped his brow with his suit jacket sleeve. "A sort of cute girl, actually."

Liz froze. She felt a little prickle of something unpleasant. "Oh, yeah?" she heard herself ask. "Did she have her face painted? She's probably a lesbian."

"Um . . . oh. I guess she is." Will grinned, puzzled. "Hey, are you all right?"

"Yeah." Liz nodded. The problem was—

Well, she didn't want to *admit* the problem: she was scared of drugs. Particularly drugs you couldn't smoke. Yes. That was it. That was why her heart had just skipped a beat. It had nothing to do with Will. There was just something about a blank little white pill that promised so much. . . . It was so *unpredictable*. What if it were aspirin? What if she had a seizure? What if she lost all control around Will and wound up doing something she would regret for the rest of her life?

"It won't turn you into a sex-crazed maniac or anything," Will said. "You know, if that's what you're worried about."

Liz laughed. "What if I want to turn into a sex-crazed maniac?"

Will's bangs flopped back in his face. "Well—I . . . Jeez, I don't know. . . . I mean, I doubt it would *hurt*."

"You're on." She reached for the pill.

Will pulled his hand out of the way. "No, no, no," he said with an impish smile. "First you have to answer three questions."

"Wi-i-i-ll," she groaned. "Come on. Before I change my mind—"

"One: Who was that big scary guy you were talking to a few minutes ago?"

She smirked and put her hands on her hips. "Robby. Next?"

Will nodded, seeming to understand. "So *that's* Robby," he murmured. "The girl who sold me these said, 'Robby was once my mortal enemy. Now we complain together in the bathosphere.'"

Liz laughed. "What's the bathosphere?"

"It's this weird circular room they built at the bottom of the smokestack, where everybody goes to complain, and the sound of their voices echoes in a really cool way. That cute girl showed it to me, actually—"

"And what's the second thing you wanted to ask?" Liz interrupted, feeling that uncomfortable and inexplicable prickle again.

"It's just something that's been bothering me ever since Dad died. Well, not *bothering* me, but just making me curious. How is he technically Jewish? Were his parents Jewish? My mom doesn't know either. I asked her about it before I came down here, and she just looked at me like I was on drugs."

"Were you?"

"Well, yeah, but still, the question is valid," he said dryly. "I feel entitled to an answer. Don't you?"

"Absolutely," Liz said, and the prickle vanished in the wake of a rush of anticipation and adrenaline. *This is going to be fun.* She eyed the pills in Will's palm. "I think Dad made the whole thing up. I think he just wanted to be buried as fast as he could after he died, and he knew that Jews bury their dead fast. You know, within twenty-four hours. I mean, obviously he knew that old rabbi guy, and he probably made some donations to the guy's synagogue. I think he did it because he was worried that if he wasn't buried fast, Mom might do some weird ritual with the SPIRIT or whatever, and that wasn't his style." She hesitated. "Weird. That whole explanation occurred to me just now, just as I was saying it. It was sort of stream of consciousness."

"We'll get to your consciousness in a second. But before we do . . . here's number three. Drumroll, please! Are you really going to date that fat kid from Kyle's web site?"

Liz laughed. "Will, we've had this conversation before. And I've told you: you can believe in whatever you want. You can even believe in a lie. You *should* believe in lies, because they're sweet and easy." She held out her own hand, brushing her fingers against Will's chest. "So, can I take this pill or what?"

chapter 16

(ONLY ABOUT THIRTY-FIVE
MINUTES), IN WHICH WILL
IS CONFRONTED WITH A
TANTALIZING CLUE AS TO
WHY HIS FATHER ACTED
THE WAY HE DID

*This place is bizarre-o Wiltshire.
It's Wednesday, and they're all at
a party on a school night!*

Tingly warmth welled up
inside Will. He ground his teeth
together. He rubbed the sides of his arms with his palms. A
wondrous chill ran down his spine. The E he'd scored from that
cute little tweaker was starting to kick in! (The good part: only
five dollars a hit for two hits. The bad part: his last ten dollars.)
Liz's hair . . . There was a purple hue. How could she go on a
date with Fat Dog? But it couldn't be a real date. That part was
definitely a lie. She'd just wanted to help Kyle for some reason—a reason that Will would probably never understand, and
it wasn't his business anyway, even though he was desperately

curious. At this point, he wasn't even jealous of Fat Dog. At least Fat Dog owned shoes. This Robby character, however . . . he went barefoot. A lot of the kids here went barefoot.

Liz wandered toward a very frightening-looking spiral staircase.

Will followed her. He didn't trust himself to speak. The first wave of the E rush was always the hardest to navigate. And this place really *did* feel like Wiltshire, that very first day. He'd been transported to a parallel, swirling-soup, MDMA-infused universe of sensations and warmth and buzzing. While none of the kids had braces (or shoes), many did have zits. While none of them looked at him like he was week-old salad, they did giggle at the lopsided peace sign on his lapel. He giggled too. A chant echoed off the happy walls of his skull: *"Euphoric, narcotic, pleasantly hallucinant . . . Euphoric, narcotic, pleasantly hallucinant . . ."*

Where did that come from?

He paused for a moment in the hall. It was on the tip of his tongue. . . . There was another great line too: *"All the advantages of Christianity and alcohol; none of their defects . . ." "Aha!"* he said out loud.

Liz turned around. "What?"

"Uh . . ." He couldn't finish. Her eyes were so big and black! He shook his head, still not confident enough to form actual words. He nodded toward the stairwell. But he'd recovered another memory—an extremely important memory—because it involved Wiltshire, and Liz, and all the other thoughts he'd had in the last five minutes.

I'm not THAT far gone . . . . *YET.*

The memory was this:

When he went to lunch that Monday (just two days ago!), at that bar O'Schtink's or whatever, he'd stopped by a Barnes & Noble on the way, and he'd picked up a copy of *Brave New World*. Not only did he want to read it (so as to avoid feeling like the only ignoramus in Ms. Thompson's class), but he'd wanted to see for himself if it embodied those themes she'd written on the board: lying, cheating, stealing, and screwing.

Indeed it had. And in subtle ways. And an added bonus: Ms. Thompson had mentioned that the author was a drug addict. Or maybe that he'd inspired drug addicts? She'd said something about Jim Morrison, anyway—about how the Doors were named after an Aldous Huxley book or quote: *The Doors of Perception.*

It didn't matter. What mattered: Will had pored over the pages while scarfing down a burger and draining three V&Ts, and he'd made it as far as the end of chapter 3 . . . and up until then it was a rollicking good tale of society-gone-bad, particularly in regard to promiscuity, consumption, and dehumanization . . . and the motto of the future One World State was "COMMUNITY, IDENTITY, STABILITY."

And that's exactly what they have here! Will cried to himself. He rubbed arms and ground his teeth and stared at purple-hued Liz hair. *That's what I was thinking about! Except it isn't bad! It's not a dystopia! Thanks to Liz!* And as his leaden feet moved further toward the stairs, he remembered even MORE CLEARLY that third and final chapter he'd read of *Brave New World*, over that third and final V&T

. . . and it was nothing more a than a rapid montage of quotes—but it was PERFECT, just little snippets of strangers' conversations, like the kind you'd overhear on the street as you passed people . . . *mots trouvées* (as they said in French class at S——: "found words"), little sparks that set off a thousand firecrackers in your brain . . . and Will opened up his ears as wide as they could go and shut his eyes, so he couldn't even tell who was doing the talking (boy? girl? hermaphrodite?). . . . He soaked in every last detail as the crowd swarmed and buzzed around him carrying on a dozen different nonsequential conversations.

". . . I can't go to the karaoke room. It's a rehab thing. Music is a trigger for me."

"They stole her identity."

"Human beings are the only organisms on the planet that beat off in secret."

"Travis has to stop Googling himself."

"The more Robby says it in a bad way, the more he wants to be it."

"I made out with an eighty-year-old once."

"Blow jobs are the new sex."

"A base of loosely organized cells, each acting on its own . . ."

"Poverty is the new wealth. . . ."

"She said I was premature. I told her I was preemptive."

"People would IM me and they'd tell me rumors they'd spread. They made up really gross stuff, too. Then there was my blog. And the only reason I started it was because my uncle was killed on nine-eleven. I mean, can you believe the stuff these assholes were saying about me? I got, like, seriously suicidal. I kept ditching school. . . ."

Will honed in on that last little snippet; honed with all his might. But it was too elusive . . . the voice faded, and then it was gone—and it left a very jittery hole in its place.

Those words, those freaking *words: uncle . . . 9/11 . . . suicidal . . . ditching . . .* They, too, were ingredients in a swirling soup, and they melted into a single foul color, leaving Will with an E-fueled conclusion: *Pete might have accidentally killed himself on purpose after all.* And he remembered something else—

He'd also ditched school the morning of 9/11. He'd ditched to hang out with Uncle Pete. He'd totally forgotten that.

Actually, that was a lie. And he knew it. He hadn't forgotten it at all. He remembered it very well, but he wanted to forget it. It was the worst memory of all time, aside from Pete's blowing himself up in the E-Z-Lern car, and he tried to forget it when he remembered, or at least to pretend to forget.

It was the second day of eighth grade.

Pete had started a new job the previous day—Monday, September 10, 2001. He'd been hired as a staff writer for the *Village Voice*, to write reviews for new bars. A dream come true. Getting paid to write about bars. It was Pete's first real job ever.

It lasted less than four hours. His boss caught him pouring Cointreau into his coffee after lunch. She threw a fit and told him, in not-so-polite terms, to leave.

Later that afternoon, Pete called Will's mom.

Will was just getting home from school, so he picked up the phone first.

Will: Hello?

Pete: Will? Is your mom around?

Will: Hey, Uncle Pete, is that you? I think so. Hold on—

Pete: No, wait!

Will: Why? Is everything all right? You sound funny.

Pete: I've had a few drinks. Look, don't get your mom. I got fired for . . . well, for starting early. Just do me a favor. Swing by my place on your way to school tomorrow, okay? I'll have doughnuts. I want to talk about this with you before I try to talk to your mom about it. You handle her better than I do.

Will hung up, feeling nervous. Doughnuts? Pete had never offered him doughnuts.

On the morning of September 11, 2001, Will arrived at Pete's place to the sound of a violent explosion: *BOOOOOM!*

"Hey, did you hear that?" Pete asked.

"Maybe a water tower fell off a building," Will said.

Pete turned on the TV. There was a flaming black hole in one of the World Trade Center towers, ten blocks away. Apparently, a small plane had crashed into it. Pete put on a pot of coffee and poured some Cointreau into an empty cup, then slurped down the cup of Cointreau without adding the coffee.

"That's fucked up," he said.

Will couldn't tell if Pete was talking about his scary alcoholism or the fact that a plane had crashed into the World Trade Center. So he kept quiet. They both did. There were no doughnuts. Sixteen minutes later—as Will sipped a cup of decaf hazelnut that tasted like sludgy horse manure and debated how to make a graceful exit—he watched on TV as another plane slammed into the other World Trade Center tower. There was a weird two-second delay between the flash on the screen and the blast. It was much louder this time, a thunderclap: *BOOOOOOOOOM!* It reverberated for nearly half a minute. The force of the impact rattled Pete's furniture. Coffee splashed on Will's hand.

Pete burst into tears. Will stared out the window. Flaming debris and scraps of white paper rained from the bright blue sky. Fire engines wailed. Will felt a peculiar foreboding. *This is bad,* he said to himself. It couldn't have been a coincidence that *two* planes had hit the World Trade Center, could it? Whatever. He should probably get out of this neighborhood. His school was nearby. For all he knew, the fire from the crashes might spread to Pete's block and to school and beyond.

"Let's go to your place," Pete said.

"I was just thinking that," Will agreed.

By the time they reached Will's place, the World Trade Center no longer existed. As to the fate of Will's school and Pete's apartment, they had no clue. All of lower Manhattan was shrouded in a toxic yellow cloud.

Will began to get more nervous. Pete began to get hysterical. This wasn't just bad; it was apocalyptic. They turned on the TV again. The reporters spoke in shaken monotones, repeating non sequiturs such as, "Um . . . radical Islam," and, "Ah . . . USS Cole," but never dispensing any worthwhile information, such as why planes were crashing into buildings. Will spent the rest of the morning frantically trying to convince Pete (and himself) that there was nothing to worry about. He'd never seen Pete cry. He'd never really seen Pete do much of anything—except drink, or complain about being overworked (odd, seeing as he'd never had a job until yesterday), or laugh about his growing credit card debt, or whisper dirtily about some fat chick he'd met at a bar.

Pete decided to call his apartment to make sure it was still standing. If the machine picked up, he figured he was in good shape. There was no dial tone. He hung up and said, "Will, I think my apartment has been swallowed in fire." Will resorted to squeezing Pete in a wordless bear hug so tight that his right leg fell asleep. (As it turned out, Pete's apartment was relatively unscathed, though it had been bathed in soot and ash. The detoxification process took three weeks. The Red Cross ended up paying for Pete to stay at the Soho Grand Hotel, where he went on a three-week bender.)

A little while later, Mom walked in. "Wild out there, huh?" she muttered. She dropped her keys into the dish—almost breezily, as if it were perfectly natural that Armageddon would be unfolding a mile away. For a few minutes, she and Will discussed the reports that a total of eight passenger jets were still aloft and unaccounted for and that the State Department was supposedly due to explode at any second. Then she asked Will why he was hugging Pete, seeing as Pete should have been at work.

Pete told her he got fired for drinking.

"That figures," she said. "On the bright side, I guess it doesn't matter much now." She turned to Will and smiled shakily, her eyes finally moistening. "And what's your excuse, honey? Shouldn't you be at school?"

"I guess."

"Don't worry about it. I'll homeschool today. But first I'll fix us all a drink."

* * *

Then—the memory was over.

Will opened his eyes. He'd forgotten the goal: *Maintain semblance of sanity at all costs. Do not let the E get on top of you.* And in spite of teeth-gnashing and temperature fluctuation and the way Liz was holding his hand—except Liz *wasn't* holding his hand. It was that same pale, starry-eyed, cute little waif who'd sold him the E. She weighed ninety pounds. She wore a wife beater and jeans and a nice thick black belt that was kind of hot, especially since her jeans rode so low under her belly button.

"Sorry!" Will yelled, jerking his hand away.

"Sorry for what?" the girl asked.

"Will?"

It was Liz's voice. The girl ran off. He watched her go, watching the echoing trail of purple light in her wake: *Sha-Na-Na-Na-Na-Na-Na . . . .*

"Did you just say you were sorry?" Liz asked, her head swimming into view.

Will shook his head and licked his dry lips. "I don't know," he gasped.

"I thought you did." Liz's cheeks were dewy. Her pupils were two big black balloons. Her dress was even blacker . . . black against her white neck. And he knew that he needed to hug someone right now—to hug someone as tightly as he'd hugged Uncle Pete that awful, awful day. He needed to hug someone he *loved*. He couldn't help himself. He swept her into an embrace. *Please don't push me away.*

She hugged him back, her fingers like spiders on his back.

"That feels so good," she whispered.

"It . . . thank God."

"That girl was trying to hit on you, I think," Liz said.

He laughed.

"What's funny?" she whispered.

"I just—I wouldn't even know how to deal with that." He squeezed his eyes closed as tightly as they would go. "I haven't hooked up with anyone since right after my uncle Pete's funeral. And that really didn't even count. She was this college chick—"

"I know," Liz breathed. Her nose nuzzled his ear. Her body shuddered. "I read your application for Wiltshire. Dad showed it to me."

Will's lids fluttered open. Somewhere in his brain, an alarm went off. He wasn't quite sure why, but it was enough to make him step back, even though he'd never wanted to cling to someone so badly in his life. "You what?"

"Don't go!" Liz seized him and yanked him against her. "Dad gave it to me. I'll tell . . . I'll tell you about it sometime. When I'm not as shivery or thirsty."

Will closed his eyes again. "When? When did he show it to you?"

"Right before he died," Liz whispered. "Let's not talk about it. Can I tell you something? I'm so glad I met you. Finally."

"Me too," Will breathed back. He could feel her hands on his back, her legs intertwined with his. "I need . . . I just—it was time for us to meet, you know? I think I figured something out, too."

"What's that?"

I think I figured out that my uncle might have killed himself on purpose because he was so monumentally traumatized and depressed, he answered silently. But he didn't really feel like sharing that with Liz. At least, not right this second.

"We need more boys like you at my school. Crazy boys. Interesting boys." Liz exhaled, nuzzling into his shoulder. "It was *meant* for us to meet, right? Not that I believe that, but because it's a lie, I *do* believe it. . . . " She and Will laughed at the same time. "I'm going to write about this," she whispered.

"Why?"

"Because it's important. Also, because I want to be famous." She giggled.

"You do?"

"Yes! Everybody wants to be famous."

"I don't," Will said with a breathless sigh. "I just want to hang out with you and with my uncle Pete during the seventies—well, mostly you . . . and a bunch of other stuff I shouldn't talk about." He stepped apart from her.

"You don't have to talk about it." She closed her eyes and drew him close once more. "You know why? You make your own choices. You never let anything or anyone choose things for you, Will. And that's why I love you."

A beatific smile formed on Will's face. It might have been the greatest lie ever told, so he knew could believe in it. And miraculously, that was when it happened. He finally conjured Pete from the dead. The flaccid old drunk stood before him, enveloped in a saintly glow, and he repeated word for word the pearls of wisdom he'd shared with Will last Christmas. *"We'd rather let the TV choose things and be things for us. And that's cool. Because on TV, everything always works out nicely and usually right after a deodorant commercial."*

Then, as fast as he'd appeared, he vanished, leaving only Liz in his place. Will had Pete's blessing. He was gone; Liz was here. Liz could help him work through this.

So he kissed her on the cheek.

She laughed inaudibly. She almost seemed to be expecting it. Her eyes still closed, she kissed him once back on the cheek: a quick peck.

Will waited for more. It wasn't enough. He'd just been to hell again. It was too detached, too dry; her lips felt like sandpaper. He didn't need dryness right now. He needed love, the love she'd just invoked. *That's why I love you.* He reached behind her head and ran his fingers through her matted blond hair.

She swallowed, never opening her eyes, never even fluttering her eyelids. "Your hand is trembling," she whispered.

"It is . . . ?" He drew her head toward his own and allowed his lips to melt against hers until they weren't dry anymore, and there was no danger of detachment.

chapter 17

Kyle sniffed his armpits.

Nice. On top of everything else, he stank.

Objectively:

He sat on a floor. Where? In a barren room. Lit with what? A lone dangling lightbulb over a painting on a wall. The painting? A life-size portrait of Jesus (white robes, crown of thorns, halo, the works) pointing a gun straight at Kyle, with a caption reading, *Give me your money, asshole!!!*

This was not a hallucination. This was fact.

This is what I've been staring at for the last half hour.

In all fairness, though, the opposite wall featured a painting of a horned devil raising his hands in fear and saying, *Don't shoot!!!* So good was balanced with evil. Or vice versa. And the paintings were skillfully rendered. Kyle was no judge of art, but they were a lot better than the average bathroom graffiti at Dorchester—pretty remarkable, seeing as this burnt-out hellhole was a long way from boarding school.

Objectively:

The only reasons he'd allowed himself to be dragged in here were because he was thirsty and hungry and to find Liz. That African American girl had promised him some water (and where was she, anyway?), and Liz owed him a snack. He very much wanted that water and that snack. He very much wanted to discuss this whole business of Fat Dog and Dad and Will with his sister, *alone*, away from Will—

The door flew open.

"Sorry it took me so long!" The skinny African American girl bounded into the room, panting and waving a bottle of Evian over her head. "I found your friends. You have to come with me! Come on, sweetheart!" She dove forward and grabbed him. Once again, he resisted; once again, she tugged; once again, he acquiesced. They had their little playacting down to a science now. She dragged him out of the room and down the hall, toward a very unsound-looking spiral staircase.

"This doesn't look safe," Kyle said.

"It isn't," the girl replied. Her grip tightened on his wrist. "Follow my footsteps exactly, okay? I mean *exactly*."

"What if I don't?"

She turned to him. "Why are you getting all hardheaded on me?" she chided in her sweet, lilting, mellifluous southern accent.

"Is there any chance I could die?"

"Sugarplum, you crack me up! There's *always* a chance you could die!"

That was a good point. What choice did he have? He followed her as carefully as he could—over holes and tacks and places where the carpet was torn or missing—but he would have followed her step for step anyway because he would not be "hardheaded." (Great term.) He would not take his sour mood out on this strange girl, who was only trying to do him a favor. Three days ago, he might have. Not now.

The girl paused in front of a door near the landing. The second floor was much more sparsely populated than the first. Kyle strained his ears. From behind the door, he could hear faint music. It was familiar, catchy. He knew it. He frowned at the door, which looked to be made of lead: it was metal and black and very thick. Scribbled on it, in what looked like glue or Liquid Paper, was the following:

COALITION OF THE CHILLING

COALITION OF THE DRILLING

COALITION OF THE FILLING

COALITION OF THE GRILLING

COALITION OF THE ILLING

COALITION OF THE KILLING

COALITION OF THE TRILLING

"Your friends are in here," she said. She swung the door forward, as if she were opening a vault.

Inside—specifically, inside what looked to be a former sweatshop, complete with rows of sewing tables—Will and Liz were slow dancing next to a big yellow karaoke machine. One of Will's hands was draped over Liz's behind. The other was stroking her hair. As for Liz . . . she had both of her hands shoved into Will's back pockets. Her eyes were closed, her head resting on his bony shoulder.

Kyle stopped breathing. "Those aren't my friends," he croaked.

"What did you say?" the girl asked.

"They're my sister and my . . ." He didn't finish.

Only then did the song's title register, somewhere deep inside his skull: "Summer Lovin'," from the musical *Grease*. Kyle knew it well because he'd seen the movie. He'd seen it with Liz and Dad, not long after Dad had taken them to see *Cats* and *Fiddler on the Roof* and a host of other musicals when they were kids. Odd: Dad's "musicals" phase had occurred during a short period of time and for no reason Kyle could ever discern other than that Dad might have wanted to get out of the house. Or he'd tried a new drug.

About two dozen other kids were slow dancing too.

They were invisible. Kyle saw only Will and Liz. He glanced back at the girl who had brought him to this place. She was gone. In her place was a folding tray with a plate of homemade chocolate chip cookies. Interesting.

He turned again to Will and Liz.

There were certain actions he could take (throwing Will to the floor and stomping on his face, maybe), but he didn't want to cause a scene. He could save that for the car. Best to con-serve energy. Best to remain objective. Best to concentrate on what he knew, not what he felt—and he *knew* he had to remove Liz from the premises. He didn't understand where this behavior was coming from. Was she *that* pissed about the Fat Dog thing? Was she that passive-aggressive? If she was, she shouldn't have volunteered to go on a date with the son of a bitch. It was her fault.

The song reached its climax: two voices in perfect harmony, male and female.

Kyle's eyes flashed to the plate of cookies. He was starving. The whole reason they'd gotten off the highway in the first place was to get something to *eat*. Of course, the cookies were probably laced—with LSD, or carpet cleaner, or worse. He grabbed one and sniffed at it, slowly rotating it under his nose. A few kids stared at him. He glared back. *Mind your own busi-ness.* His mouth watered. The cookie didn't smell laced. But who could tell? If he lost his mind or overdosed, Liz would bear the responsibility. She would have to live with the guilt of hav-ing led him into this nightmare in the first place. It would serve her right. It was almost worth the risk of an overdose. He wolfed down the whole cookie in three seconds and stormed over to her.

"Hi!" he spat. Crumbs dribbled from his chin.

Neither Liz nor Will budged. They didn't even open their eyes.

Kyle grabbed Liz's shoulder and wrenched her away from Will.

"Hey!" she protested. She blinked, as if waking up from a nap.

"What do you think you're doing?" Kyle demanded.

"We're da-a-ancing," Will slurred.

Kyle jerked a finger in his face. "Shut up. I'm not talking to you. Liz?"

"We're . . . dancing," she repeated, backing away.

"Liz, are you on drugs right now? That's what I'm hoping. Otherwise, I can't see why you'd be hitting on your own brother a day after your father died."

Liz froze. Her eyes went wide and black. There: it was now out in the open. There: it was met with silence. The music stopped. A couple of kids whispered; some giggled: all of them began to hurry out of the room. Now if only Will would follow those kids—and maybe plunge through the spiral staircase on his way down and die a horrible death; that would certainly help matters. Then Kyle could finally be alone with his twin.

"Well?" he pressed. The seconds ticked by in excruciating silence.

"Kyle," Liz began. "I—" She broke off.

A very intimidating, very muscular bald guy marched through the door. He wore a wife-beater tank top. Both forearms were obscured by fiendish tattoos. A hideous red scar marred his scalp. He looked like a Nazi.

"Hi, y'all," he said. His voice was at least twice as deep as Kyle's.

"Hey, Robby," Liz and Will answered at the same time.

Kyle almost had to laugh. "So this is the famous Robby. Perfect timing."

"I'm sorry, but I'm gonna have to ask y'all to leave," Robby stated.

Kyle glared at him. "What? Why?"

"Somebody just told me there was fighting up here," he said.

"Oh my God, Robby, I'm so sorry," Liz apologized, edging away from Will (thankfully). "This is just a family squabble, you know? We're just working some stuff out. It's not a real fight. Kyle just gets mad and he puts on this attitude—"

"All the same, I'm going to have to ask you to leave," Robby interrupted.

"We should probably be getting back on the road anyway," Will mumbled.

"We're really sorry," Liz kept jabbering. "We'll be out of here in a second."

"Shut up!" Kyle shouted, his control ebbing away. He thrust a finger toward Robby, his body hot and tensed, positioning himself right in front of him. "You've used my web site without my permission, you know that?"

Robby smiled. It was a little frightening—particularly because it was so nonthreatening. Maybe Kyle should relax. The contrast between this guy's peaceful demeanor and overall appearance was a little too much.

"I linked to your site," Robby said contritely. "I didn't know you wanted me to get permission. If it's a problem, I'll remove the link. Now, if you'll please just get out."

"Jesus, Kyle," Liz whispered. "You're ruining everything!"

Kyle raised a finger at her, keeping his eyes on Robby.

"I'm not the one who's trying to hook up with a sibling. I'm not the one—"

"*You* shut up!" Liz cried. She ran from the room.

"Liz!" Will shouted, fast on her heels.

Robby turned and hurried after them both.

Kyle hesitated. One moment, he was in a room full of people; the next, he was alone. What famous philosopher said, *Hell is other people?* Jean-Paul Sartre? Yeah . . . that sounded right. Was he also the guy who said, *Every human being is alone?* Maybe. Or maybe Kyle just made that up right now. . . . He hurried out the door to the top of the stairwell.

Will and Liz were already gone. *Shit.* Robby bounded back upstairs with surprising agility—two steps at a time—and before Kyle could fight back, Robby heaved him over his shoulder like a sack of potatoes. In truth, Kyle felt a strange measure of relief . . . even as blood rushed to his face and his gut mashed against Robby's shoulder: he trusted Robby to navigate the stairs much better than he could. But Robby didn't stop at the bottom of the stairwell. He rushed Kyle straight out the door, past those four sweaty guys in black turtlenecks, and then gently propped him up on his feet.

"Go on, kid," Robby said, breathing hard. "Go find your sister."

Kyle caught a glimpse of Will, disappearing into the shadows across the field.

"We're sorry, Robby!" Will called.

"What are you waiting for?" Robby asked.

Kyle shook his head. "I don't know."

"Then get going."

"Right. Sorry." Kyle took a deep breath and ran too. He chased after Will as fast as he could, praying that Liz hadn't fallen into a ditch or been gobbled up by an alligator—but he couldn't help but steal a last quick peek over his shoulder at Robby's bulky silhouette in the entranceway. And he wondered what it would be like to look and act like Robby did, to project that peaceful, war-like dichotomy and that absolute authority . . . the kind of authority that could make even someone like Kyle run.

It would probably help out a lot with the crap he needed to deal with in his life.

* * *

Thank God—it took less than a minute to find Liz.

Will had followed her footsteps (the trampled grass showed up pretty well in the moonlight), and Kyle had followed *his* footsteps . . . and now, here they were. She'd simply reached the end of the field and tumbled down an embankment into some scrub brush, where she'd decided to stay. Was there a creek bed down there? Kyle wasn't sure. He could hear her, though, sniffling somewhere very close in the black abyss.

"The trick is to avoid the holes," Will said as he crept over the precipice.

What holes? What the hell are you talking about? Kyle

glanced back toward the factory. Robby was gone. The relief he felt at having found Liz so fast quickly morphed into something else . . . a strange sort of excitement—because now that they had found her, she was the last thing he wanted to think about. He definitely didn't want to think about her and Will. He wanted to shut them both out of his mind. Yes, instead, he'd rather think about . . . well, this little factory here. This place was an untapped gold mine.

He started to smile. A vision flashed before him, prepackaged and ready-made: hundreds of Kyle Shepherd New Democracy Gatherings™ all across the country—all across the whole wide *world*—cost-effective events where kids could feel free to let loose and do whatever they wanted: dance, facepaint, perform karaoke—everything EXCEPT hook up with siblings—and all for a low, low price . . . five bucks admission, tops. He could even get that skinny African American girl to do the ads. "What's a Kyle Shepherd Gathering of the New Democracy™?" somebody would ask. "It's whatever you want it to be," she would reply in that sultry voice. (Although she might want to lose the ironic WHITE TRASH AND PROWD OF IT!!! T-shirt. He didn't want to offend any consumers.)

Boom. Done.

Forget a thirty-seventy split with Fat Dog. Screw it. Fat Dog could *have* prepdate.com. "Help the Heroes!" too. Kyle was going to take *this* shit into the millions. Damn straight. He was going to *get* something out of this awful—

"Liz?" Will called, stumbling down into the shadows. "Liz? Can you hear me?"

"Yes, I can, Will," she answered. She sounded very small and far away.

Kyle squinted down the embankment. He couldn't see a damn thing.

"Give me your hand," Will said, his voice uncertain and drug-soaked. "There you go, Liz, right. Grab hold."

From the darkness, the two of them emerged, scrambling back, hand in hand, onto the field.

"Are you okay?" Will gasped.

"That's a funny question, Will," Liz panted.

Will smiled, then stopped.

Their eyes met. They both turned away, their faces sickly.

Liz shook free of Will's hand. "Listen, Kyle, I'm sorry I ran like that," she said. She looped her arm through Kyle's and dragged him back toward the factory, deliberately leaving Will to walk on his own. Kyle wasn't sure if that was good or bad. It seemed *too* deliberate . . . as if she were scared of what might happen if she touched Will again. Besides, he wasn't pissed that she'd run; he was pissed . . . for another reason. Their footsteps crunched in the dry grass. "I guess I'm just sort of wasted," Liz went on. "I mean, this is the very first time I've ever done E. . . . You know that, but I'm just—" She jerked to a stop. She pointed into the darkness. "Oh my God!"

Kyle peered in the direction of her outstretched hand. *Holy—*

Somebody had painted a giant peace sign on the hood of the Volvo.

Will started to giggle.

Remarkably, Kyle didn't even feel that upset. There was no point in discussing it. A little vandalism—so what? There was no point in discussing *anything*, other than how he planned to make money off the New Democracy. If Liz didn't want to talk about the Will situation, then he didn't want to either. He would ignore it until New York. Just like he would ignore this graffiti. With both Liz and Will in the car, he could *control* it, too. Then, after New York, Will would be gone forever. Why harp on something so unpleasant and disgusting? Kyle trudged forward and unlocked the doors. The three of them piled in. Will sprawled out in the backseat again. Kyle's nose wrinkled. The car stank.

He stuck the key into the ignition and then turned to Liz.

"Listen, I have this idea," he said before he started the engine. "What if I came back down here and apologized to Robby? You know, over Columbus Day? What if I got him all excited about prepdate.com? Then, what if he and I used prepdate.com to start spreading the word about this Gathering of the New Democracy thing? Fat Dog says we've got a lot of visibility right now. And with a little start-up capital, I could take these gatherings all across the country. Robby and I could become partners. We could, you know . . . *franchise* this." He took a deep breath. He had no idea where that diatribe had come from. But it felt good to say it. It felt *really* good.

"You're kidding, right?" Liz asked, fastening her seat belt.

"No. Why?"

"Kyle, that's the worst freaking idea I ever heard!" Will croaked from the backseat. "I mean, come on! When you franchise something, it becomes corrupt. Worse. It becomes a McDonald's or a Wal-Mart. You want to turn this factory into a Wal-Mart? You gotta leave things like this alone. Unspoiled. Unpackaged. Unbranded. Just think of what Dad said today. I mean, for real . . . if you franchised the Gathering of the New Democracy, you wouldn't be working *for* The Man, you'd BE The Man."

"Exactly," Liz concurred.

Kyle didn't answer right away. "So?" he finally asked. "What's the problem?"

"Kyle, if you don't know the answer to that question," Liz said, "then you're worse off than I thought."

"I probably am," Kyle agreed. "But Liz? You understand you just flipped out and ran off into a swamp, don't you? Plus, you're siding with a disturbed, drunken loser who's let his entire life pass him by up until this point. You're more than siding. You're . . ." His jaw clenched. "Whatever. You do understand that, don't you?"

Liz winced. "Jesus, Kyle."

Kyle turned toward the backseat.

Will's eyes were closed. Apparently, within the last five seconds, he'd managed to pass out. He probably hadn't even heard that little jab. Kyle started the engine. He pulled out of the field and back into the swamp, a lump forming in his throat. Too bad Dad wasn't here. Although he definitely would have sided with Will on the whole franchising of the New Democracy issue. . . .

"Why are you so pissed, Kyle?" Liz asked. "You're the one who got us kicked out of there. And *I'm* the one who's going on a date with Fat Dog, remember?"

Kyle tried to swallow the lump. It wouldn't go away. "I'm pissed," he finally managed, easing his foot down on the accelerator, "because we should have been teaching Will how to drive instead taking a detour to do drugs and dance and—why *did* you do drugs tonight, Liz? You scared the shit out of me!"

"Yeah, well, I'm sorry about that. But as far as coming here goes, I thought we were out of gas. Isn't that what you said? We might as well have stopped somewhere."

"We *are* out of gas. We're going to a gas station right now."

"Kyle, I really am sorry for running away like that. I swear it'll never happen again. I didn't want to scare you. I was just . . . I was just wasted. I still am."

"No kidding."

"But you have to promise me something."

Kyle gazed at the flickering swampland ahead of him. "I do?"

"You have to promise me you'll help Will get that two million. We'll teach Will how to drive as soon as we sober up. We have plenty of time. As long as you and I work together, I swear I'll never run off like that again. I won't ask for any more detours, and I won't dance with Will anymore—" She bit her lip. "You know . . . if dancing came up."

"You really think we can teach Will to drive in time?"

"I know we can," she said.

Kyle sniffed. "Sure. We have less than thirty hours, Liz. And this is a stick."

chapter 18

(THE REMAINDER OF THAT NIGHT, WITH A CONSPICUOUS GAP LEADING INTO THE NEXT MORNING), IN WHICH WILL ATTEMPTS TO LEARN TO DRIVE

Contrary to Kyle's belief, Will had not passed out. He stretched flat on his back, his eyes tightly shut, his brain both asleep and awake. He'd reached that darkly magical, elusive equilibrium—the electrifying precipice where a person could tumble down from sanity into insanity and, beyond that, into something far more dangerous . . . but the car's vibrations were as soothing as the rocking of a cradle. The night wind was like velvet on his cheek . . . the velvet of Liz's handbag. . . . There was balance.

They'd made out for almost a minute.

I made out with my half sister for almost a minute.

His heart pounded. He'd done a terrible, terrible thing.

Images danced across his eyelids. *SHA-NA-NA-NA-NA-NA*....

.... Liz in his arms, Liz shrieking with delight when they stumbled upon the karaoke room . . . *Liz, Liz, Liz*. It was wrong. It was bad. He searched inside for some feelings of revulsion, of horror—and he found them . . . but they should have been more powerful. Why did everything wicked and foul and forbidden feel so good? But maybe he shouldn't even doubt or question it. Being with Liz—making out with her or not—was like rediscovering an old hobby, a hobby he'd forgotten since Pete had blown himself up. AND she was also the first person he'd met in the past ten months who didn't treat him like "a disturbed, drunken loser who has let his entire life pass him by up until this point."

Even Dr. Brown didn't treat him so nicely.

What would it be like to make out with her for longer than a minute?

Okay: now he'd tumbled over the precipice. But that felt good too. He shouldn't have asked that question of himself. But he had. *But, but, but* . . . Making out with her again would be . . . Lips. Hair. Eyes. Until that moment, he supposed he'd intended to fry his mind to the point where he wouldn't be *able* to think about kissing her. Also to the point where he wouldn't be able to think about why Dad hated him or about why Uncle Pete crashed that car. But thanks to the chemical soup he'd ingested, and his memory of 9/11, and Murphy's Law and the second law of thermodynamics and various other universal laws (such as the law that required Will Shepherd raid the liquor cabinet when Mom met with a client), he could only think about such matters when he was the *most* fried. It was a pesky Catch-22.

Dr. Brown would no doubt have lots to say about it. In a nice way, of course.

But Will would worry about that later. For now, he was free-falling into paradise.

* * *

"Hey, Will," Kyle whispered. "Psst. Will."

Will grunted.

There was a nudge. "WILL!"

Will snapped upright. The light in his eyes . . . blinding. The drugs had inexplicably worn off. No slow expansion of pain in his skull this time; it was full-on agony. He was a newborn infant. Kyle was the ob-gyn who'd yanked him from the sanctuary of the womb. *Spank!* He felt like crying. It would be perfectly appropriate, even healthy. Every newborn cried. This wasn't a hangover. This was torture. His blood was toxic, poison, a hazmat. He squinted over at Kyle, driving beside him.

Somehow, Will had been transferred to the front passenger seat.

He had no recollection of the transfer. His seat belt was fastened.

Only then did he realize that the blinding light was the sun. Was it coming up or going down? The sky was a gruesome, post-nuclear-holocaust red. The air seemed ice cold, too, but maybe that was just because it was blasting into his face.

"What time is it?" Will choked out.

"A little after six in the morning," Kyle said. "Time for your first driving lesson. How do you feel?"

"I . . . don't know. I . . ." He shook his head. "Like death."

"Well, if you like death, you'll love driving."

With a horrifying screech, Kyle whipped across three lanes and took the next exit, hurtling down the off-ramp at twice the pre-scribed speed. Will was sure he was going to vomit. He fumbled to unclasp his seat belt and turn at the same time, hoping at least to get some of the puke on Kyle. The kid was a sadist. But at that moment, Will caught a brief glimpse of Liz, sleeping peacefully in the back-seat. He held his breath. *Bad to puke in front of Liz*, he told himself. *Bad even to look at Liz* . . . The nausea subsided a little, bowing to his sense of decency. He clutched at the door.

"Hey," Liz said groggily. "What's going on?"

"Nothing," Kyle said. "I'm gonna teach Will how to drive. Go back to sleep, all right? I'll wake you up in a few hours and we can grab some breakfast."

Liz yawned and stretched. "No, I want to help."

Kyle sped down a country road. On the left, a deserted park-ing lot swept into view. Will clutched the seat handle once again. The parking lot was behind a low-built yellow-tiled building . . . a warehouse. . . . There was a sign: COSMOS FABRICS.

"I want to help, Kyle," Liz repeated. Her eyes met Will's in the mirror. Her face whitened. She lowered her gaze, pressing up against the door so he couldn't see her.

"Fine," Kyle said. He turned into the Cosmos Fabrics park-ing lot and jerked to a stop. In a methodical fashion, he unfas-tened his seat belt, threw the door open, and stormed out of the car—leaving the motor running.

"Get in the driver's seat, Will," he commanded.

Will sat there for a few seconds. On top of the fact that Liz didn't seem to want to look at him (not that he could blame her), this was a recipe for disaster. No doubt. But he dutifully slithered to his left. It took some careful maneuvering to avoid getting goosed by the stick shift. He'd only sat behind the wheel of a car twice in his life and never with the engine on. Both times he'd been at this chick Cindy's country house, a chick from S— — who used to have parties all the time in eleventh grade, up in Connecticut when her parents were away—and both times he'd been trying to hook up with the same girl, who found it "charming" that he didn't know how to drive. Alyssa Something.

As he eased down into the cushions and stared at the dashboard, he gulped.

The dials were as incomprehensible as a foreign language. The steering wheel was much more intrusive than he remembered, too, practically jutting into his abdomen. And . . . *Hold on a second.* He looked down at his feet. There were *three* pedals down there. He'd always assumed that there were just two: the gas and the brake.

"That smaller pedal on the left is the clutch," Kyle said. "This car doesn't have an automatic transmission."

"What's an automatic transmission?" Will asked.

"Get out of the car, Liz," Kyle said, by way of response.

That comment would mark the apogee of Kyle's patience during the lesson.

* * *

For the next hour or so, Will vainly attempted to follow Kyle's enraged and bewildering instructions ("Okay, feed the engine a little gas—NOT THAT MUCH—now ease up on the clutch— NO, NO, NO—right hand on the gearshift, you idiot . . . Oh, brother . . . Stay out of this, Liz . . .") and without fail, Will failed. Liz sat on the asphalt at a safe distance, peering at the ongoing catastrophe in the morning sunshine. The only positive part of the whole experience was that the ulcer-inducing concentration it took to get the car to move at all—*simply to lurch forward*—enabled Will to blot out the burning need to get Liz alone for a few seconds and apologize or explain himself.

"Jesus, Will, stop it!" Kyle finally shouted. He waved his arms over his head and then plopped down beside Liz. "You're gonna strip the gears! You can't shift like that! Don't you know *anything*? If this car breaks down, we're screwed! You're screwed! Can't you just be a little more grown-up? You're older than I am!"

Will bowed his aching, hungover head against the steering wheel. He was developing whiplash. He started to laugh. It was pretty much all he could do at this point. How could he be expected to know anything about gearshifts?

"I'm glad you find this so funny," Kyle said.

"I'm sorry, Kyle." Will groaned.

Liz punched Kyle on the shoulder. "Lighten up a little, okay?"

"Don't touch me," Kyle barked. "You're in no condition to give me advice."

Oh God, no, Will pleaded silently. *Please don't get in another fight. Please don't bring up last night. Please just bury it and forget about it while Kyle is around. . . .*

"Kyle, can't you just see the humor in the situation?" Liz asked gently. "Can't you see the humor in trying to teach a guy how to drive in the middle of nowhere—in a beat-up Volvo with a peace sign on the hood?"

Will chuckled again, even though he really didn't want to. Mostly he chuckled because Liz wouldn't look at him. She wouldn't even *blink* in his direction.

"So this is funny to you, Will, huh?" Kyle demanded. "In case you forgot, I'm trying to help you."

"I didn't forget that, Kyle. It's still very clear in my mind. It's just that nobody's ever asked me to be 'grown-up' before. I'm not sure if the term applies yet. I mean, yes, I can vote and serve in the armed forces, but I still can't drink legally."

Kyle's face crumpled.

"So, should we get on with the lesson?" Will asked.

"I don't understand you at all," Kyle said disgustedly. "Why didn't you ever learn how to drive? Didn't you want to?"

"Nope," Will said. "Never."

It was the truth, too, and not only because of Uncle Pete. Honestly. Having lived in New York City all of his life, Will learned on his own what Uncle Pete had always insisted: that there was no need to learn to drive. Cars were a *hindrance* in Manhattan. They made people angry. Case in point: they made Kyle angry, even in an abandoned parking lot in the middle of the South on a Thursday morning. Then again, a lot of things made Kyle angry, and rightly so. But there were benefits to not driving, as Pete had sagely laid out for him. Will could be more irresponsible at parties than anybody else around (in terms of aggregate levels of irresponsibility), for the obvious reason that he would never have to chauffeur anyone. Plus, he'd never have to worry about car thieves, or insurance, or filling a gas tank, or mowing down an old lady, or incinerating himself in a fiery explosion for no apparent reason whatsoever.

Over these last years, lots of people had posited various theories as to why Will had never learned to drive, and not only Mom and Dr. Brown. Even former friends and peripheral acquaintances felt knowledgeable enough to claim that he was overanxious, paranoid, agoraphobic, alcoholic, and so on. But none of them were correct. (Well, they were, but not as specifically related to driving.)

The real reason? Ever since he'd begun to appreciate his relationship with Uncle Pete for what it truly was—that it was more than just an uncle-nephew thing, that they were best friends and kindred souls . . . no, indeed, that they were kindred SPIRITS (something he'd realized pretty much right after 9/11, when they'd really started hanging out and drinking heavily together)—Will had always felt a little too *young*, a little too *immature*, just *not grown-up enough* to take command of a high-speed motorized vehicle.

The way he saw it, more people could stand to be so cognizant of their own shortcomings. There would probably be fewer accidents.

He wished he could share that bit of wisdom with Liz. But seeing as she'd covered her face with her hands, she didn't seem much in the mood for more conversation.

part V:

THE HOMECOMING

chapter 19

It was Kyle who finally broke the silence, back on the highway.

"Liz, we really need to deal with Will's situation," he shouted over the Volvo's struggling motor. "We made the right move by giving up. We'd never be able to teach him to drive. He would have destroyed the car. Or killed us all. But we need to figure out what to do next."

Liz nodded from the backseat. Nice how Kyle spoke as if Will weren't there, wasn't it—even though Will was sitting right beside him? Dealing with Will's situation had been her idea from the start. But when *she'd* tried to deal with it, Kyle had freaked out, and then she'd taken Ecstasy, and then she'd hung out with Will, and then . . .

Don't go there. Not now.

"I say we stage some sort of accident right near Chad's office," Kyle went on. "Just a minor little fender bender. The car needs to be taken into the shop anyway to get that peace sign removed, right? So how about this? I bump into a fire hydrant somewhere in Midtown. Then I switch seats with Will. He calls the cops. He claims that some idiot cyclist or jaywalking pedestrian jumped in front of him and he swerved to avoid the guy. That way, Will Shepherd, fuck-up son, can reasonably blame an act of Providence for his failure to arrive at Chad's office. And he'll have two witnesses—you and me, Liz! We'll swear to Chad he was 'behind the wheel.'" Kyle made air quotes. "See? The car will get towed to the shop, and Chad will be none the wiser."

"But wouldn't the cops want to see my driver's license if I did that?" Will asked.

"Maybe you could say that you lost your wallet somewhere outside of New York while you were stopping to eat," Kyle suggested.

"Hey, speaking of which, can we stop for brunch?" Liz asked. "I'm starving."

This was true. The only solid food to have passed her lips in the past twenty-four hours consisted of one strange white pill that still hadn't quite worn off yet. If it *had* worn off, she wouldn't have felt this constant, nagging, desperate desire to throw Kyle out of the driver's seat (or at least get rid of him for a minute) and pull Will aside and tell him that what had happened last night could never happen again—

"I'm starving too," Kyle growled.

"I'm starving three," Will added.

"Awesome!" Liz yelled flatly. She thrust her fist in the air.

"What are you so happy about?" Kyle spat. He shot her a stony glare in the rearview mirror

She sighed, avoiding his eyes. "I'm happy that we're being honest. We've all admitted that we're hungry. It's a small thing but important. It marks the first time the three of us have all been completely honest with each other." She sat up straight. She could feel her face turning red, but she plowed forward, harnessing this fleeting honesty, milking it for all it was worth—anything not to focus on Will. "Okay, Kyle? I'm going to ask you something, and I don't care that Will is here, because he should hear it. My question is: Why aren't we close? Why *aren't* we friends?"

"What do you mean?" Kyle said.

"You know what I mean. We're twins. Twins should have some sort of inner connection—you know, beyond language, beyond *anything*. But we've never been close. Mom and Dad never dressed us in the same clothes; we don't think the same thoughts; we don't look all that much alike. . . . There's nothing that holds us together. Why is that?"

Kyle returned his eyes to the highway, one hand on the wheel, the other lazily resting atop the gearshift. "Liz?" he said, his voice quiet and measured. "I think you're still a little wasted. So just chill. You don't sound like yourself right now."

"See?" Liz slapped the upholstery. "That's what I'm talking about."

"See what?" Kyle groaned.

"I accused Will of that exact same thing," she said—

appropriating Kyle's MO of pretending Will wasn't there and not even caring about her own hypocrisy in doing so. She was on a roll now. "At the shiva, I told him he didn't sound like himself. And that was wrong. Because I don't *know* who he is, you know? I don't even know who I am! How could I? How could you? There's a new me every single day! And you know what? That's fine. I'm seventeen. How *could* I know who I am? Do *you* know who I am? Do you know who you are?"

Kyle checked his mirrors. "I guess not. But I wish I did."

Liz leaned back. "I wish I did too. And maybe I'll find out. But in the meantime, I'm happy to take questions from you two. As long as they're honest."

"What do you mean . . . honest?" Kyle asked.

"I'm instating a new rule," she said. "No more secrets."

Will tugged at his clumped bangs. "I don't know about that," he chimed in nervously. "What does that mean?"

"It'll be sort of like truth or dare, but without the dare part," Liz said.

"I'd rather just listen to the radio," Kyle muttered.

"Yes!" Will cried. He breathed a frantic sigh of relief. "Tunes! We haven't even listened to any tunes on this trip. Who the hell *are* we?"

Kyle leaned forward and snapped on the radio. There was an excruciating blast of static, then nothing. Kyle spun the dial furiously. He pressed the buttons. Silence.

"I think the radio died when the emergency gas light died," Liz pronounced. She grabbed her new laptop from under Will's seat and unzipped it, flipping it open in its case, fumbling with the power button as the car rattled. "Now, this is an important exercise. . . ."

Both Will and Kyle looked in the mirror.

"Taking notes for your memoir?" they asked at the same time. They grimaced at each other. *The drugs have definitely NOT worn off,* Liz thought. Will slumped in his seat. Kyle changed lanes, even though the highway was completely deserted.

"I'm not taking notes for my memoir," Liz said. She clicked onto the prepdate.com site. "I just want to demonstrate that people tend to be a little more honest when they can hide behind cyberspace. I want us to achieve that same level of honesty here."

Kyle stamped on the accelerator. "Who *are* you right now?"

"I don't know!" Liz yelled. "That's the whole point! You keep asking me that. And it's a good question. I guess I've been pretending to be someone, and I'm trying to find out who that is. . . ." Her fingers danced over the keyboard. She clicked onto the Prepdate Recent Comments:

10:45 a.m. i know this is like old news but still can't believe kyle's dad od'd that night! ☹!!! kyle is totally cute i hope he's ok

—stargirl446

10:47 a.m. yeah but do you think it's weird that he would even mention his dad died? i mean nobody's even hooked up since then. it's put this like morbid pall over the whole

dating and hooking-up thing. just my
opinion but what do i know???
—rxdrugs19

10:49 a.m. it wasn't kyle it was that other guy who
mentioned it. the fat guy who helps him
—stargirl446

10:51 a.m. r u sure? **—rxdrugs19**

10:52 a.m. i'm totally sure cuz there was like this bitter tone that kyle never has. . . . he is
such a hottie . . . omg . . . i just want to
hug him and console him so bad! ok i
want to do more than that. . . . hee hee!!!
—stargirl446

10:54 a.m. tmi . . . wtf . . . u r so in need of help!!! but
so am i . . . cuz why is it that death makes
us horny???? i mean it always does. . . .
—rxdrugs19

10:55 a.m. U R SO RIGHT!!!!!! TOTALLY!!!!!!
WHY??????? i mean i know this is so
twisted and everybody's gonna find out
who wrote this anyway but when my aunt
died and i went to the funeral my first

cousin looked so sad and so hot and when
i hugged him i hugged him for 2 long
—stargirl446

"Anything good there?" Kyle asked from the front seat.

Liz slammed the computer closed. "No. Nope. The server is down for some reason." She zipped up the case, her hands shaking, and shoved it under Will's seat. "I guess Fat Dog couldn't handle the upkeep while you were gone."

"So, Liz," Will said. "Are you serious about this no-more-secrets thing?"

"Sure. Of course." Her breath came fast.

"I have a question, then. You read my application essay. And Kyle, I apologize if you're lost here . . . but here's my question to you, Liz: Why do you think my uncle Pete killed himself? Because he was so depressed and fucked up after nine-eleven?"

Liz struggled to focus on the question.

It was a very good one. It deflected her thoughts from the much more troubling issues at hand—namely, that she wanted to hug Will again. Or more. So it took a little effort to formulate a response. She'd dug her own grave (ha, ha . . . lousy metaphor) with this honesty thing, and she wouldn't insult Will by bullshitting him.

"Will, from what you tell me, Pete was fucked up and depressed way before that. He might have always been suicidal and hidden it. People hide all sorts of things." She paused. "On the other hand, it could have been an accident. I really don't know him well enough to say."

Will nodded from the front seat. "Thanks," he said.

"You mean it?"

"I mean it. I'm not lying. I believe you. As in, I *honestly* believe you."

Liz waited for Kyle to say something rude or to comment on Will's fucked-up family or their mission to secure Will's inheritance.

He didn't. Instead, he concentrated on the road.

chapter 20

(TWENTY MINUTES LATER AND BEYOND), IN WHICH KYLE TRULY DISCOVERS A SIDE OF LIZ HE'S NEVER SEEN BEFORE

A little before noon, Kyle pulled into a Shorty's, some sort of southern chain diner. He'd seen about a billion signs for Shorty's during this hellish trip, and now he wanted to try it out. Fortunately, Liz and Will were in agreement. None of them spoke. They parked; they entered; they took the booth nearest the register. In order to preempt debate about the seating arrangement, Kyle seized Liz's arm to make sure that *they* sat on the same side—the twins united, across from Will, their half brother.

In Liz's new spirit of honesty, Kyle could *admit* that he didn't like the idea of Liz and Will sitting next to each other. He couldn't admit it out loud, not without provoking some sort of incident, but he could admit it to himself.

A waitress in a brown polyester uniform appeared: flabby, pasty, and about Will's age or older. Liz ordered a three-egg omelet with a side of sausage, plus home fries and toast and an orange juice. And coffee. Kyle ordered the same. Will ordered two screwdrivers and an English muffin. The waitress grinned.

"Can I see some ID, sweetheart?" she asked. *Kin ah see sum ah-dee?*

"Sure." Will pulled a tattered passport out of his back pocket, permanently warped in the shape of his left butt cheek. "Oops!" he mumbled. He shoved it back inside and hurriedly pulled out his wallet instead.

Liz laughed. So did the waitress. Kyle didn't. Passports were valuable. Will was taking a huge risk by carrying it around on him like that. Not only that—Will was using it to order booze at eleven o'clock on a Thursday morning.

Will removed an ID from his wallet and handed it to her.

"Sorry about the confusion," he said.

The waitress smiled and shook her head as she examined the card. "You sure don't look twenty-four, sugar," she mused. "But you do look like you could use a good night's rest." She turned and headed toward the kitchen.

"I think she likes you," Liz whispered to Will.

He blushed.

"Will, why do you carry your passport on you?" Kyle asked.

"I needed a real ID to fly down here," Will said. He looked

around the restaurant. "Hey, have you guys ever seen *Pulp Fiction?*"

"Oh my God," Liz whispered. She leaned across the table and then backed off. "That is so funny! I was just thinking the same thing. This diner totally reminds me of that one in the movie. You know, with that campy fifties feel? But not the diner where John Travolta and Uma Thurman eat, but the diner where John Travolta and Samuel L. Jackson go at the end? That's what you mean, right? You know what else is funny? My ex-boyfriend, Damon, *met* Quentin Tarantino." She brushed her hair out of her eyes.

Will laughed. "How did Damon meet Quentin Tarantino?"

"When he was stoned in Cabo San Lucas," Liz said.

"I wonder if he's—"

"Quentin Tarantino is a sick bastard," Kyle said, mostly to shut them up. If Liz was so into this "honesty" thing, then she should have acknowledged that she was flirting with Will (*flirting!*), which was beyond sick in its own right, and it was ruining Kyle's appetite . . . plus, they were treating him like a dud, like a third wheel, like he was some kind of hack musician trying to jam with professionals: every note he played was sour and out of tune—and worse, it sent Will and Liz off on a wild new collaborative riff . . . and how could Liz buy into Will's *shit*, anyway? Wasn't she *listening* to him?

"You know what?" Will was saying. "I think I'm gonna keep half of the two million for myself and use the other half to sponsor Iraqi and Afghan war orphans who want to move to the

States. I'm serious. In the tradition of Dad. You know, like what he did with the Vietnam war orphans."

"That is SO COOL," Liz said. "Like father, like son! What a beautiful thing! If you want, I bet we can look through Dad's old records and see how he did it. . . ."

That was it. That was more than Kyle could take.

"Will?" he barked. "Can we drop the BS for two seconds? I don't want to spend any more time with you than I have to, because unless you get your head out of your ass, *all* your money is going to those Vietnamese war orphans. So I suggest we *focus on the problem at hand*. Otherwise, I'd be happy to drop you in the gutter."

Will looked at him across the table. His face softened. He perked up, tilting his head toward the cheesy elevator music trickling from the speakers above them.

"You hear that?" he whispered.

Kyle strained his ears. It was a song from the eighties:

"It's raining men! Hallelujah!

It's raining men. . . ."

"I was almost tempted to say something," Will continued. "Well, no—now I *have* to say it, because Liz said no more secrets. But for the record: I have a sick sense of humor, and this isn't even funny to me." He drained the rest of his screwdriver and stood. "I was going to say, This song answers my question. This song tells me why Pete was so messed up after nine-eleven. Because it pretty much describes what happened in his neighborhood, and in a way Pete would have said it himself. Now, excuse me. I gotta take a leak." He hurried toward the men's room.

Liz grabbed Kyle's arm. "What the hell is your problem?

This guy is your family, whether you like it or not. *His* dad just died too, you know?"

"Excuse me?" Kyle hissed. "You're getting self-righteous with me again? You're back to Liz the grown-up? Will couldn't care less that Dad died. And I will *not* show compassion for a scumbag who wants to sleep with his own half sister. Because you're my *full* sister, my *twin* sister—whether you like it or not."

Liz's face fell. "I . . ."

Kyle stared down at his place mat. Fortunately, the waitress appeared with their food and began setting the heaping plates of steaming, greasy, fried fat in front of them, so they *couldn't* talk. As soon as she left, Liz leaned over.

"If you could just stop thinking about yourself for a second, you would see that I'm trying to help Will through this," she whispered, her nose less than three inches from Kyle's. "Think about it! Dad is tormenting him from beyond the grave! He's tormenting all of us! He's making Will jump through impossible hoops for a despicable little chunk of change. I'm trying to be *nice* to him because his life is in a free fall."

"You're lying, Liz! You *like* him. You do. You—"

Ding ding dong. Ding-de-de ding ding dong . . .

Liz's cell phone was ringing. *Oh, brother.* (The tone was a Dr. Dre sample from 1992 or something.) For a second, she almost looked happy. Kyle scrunched his mottled suit pant legs. Maybe he'd been a little harsh. Or not. The truth was, he felt bad for Will too: Dad wanted to give his own son's money to war orphans he'd never even *met.*

"I wonder if that's Brit or Mercedes." Liz pulled the phone

out of her velvet bag and flipped it open, clearly not recognizing the number. "Hello? Yes. Who's this?"

"Who is it?" Kyle asked.

Liz clamped her hand over the mouthpiece. "Fat Dog," she whispered.

"Fat Dog!" Kyle shouted. White-hot fury flashed through him. He dove for the phone, but Liz jerked away.

"Yeah?" she asked, hopping out of the booth. She paced back and forth in front of it. "Yeah . . . I figured you saw that. And I know you spoke to Kyle. Listen, man, I'll go out with you to a movie or something, but not if you blackmail my brother. Kyle deserves his fair share. . . ."

Kyle flopped back in the seat, staring at her. She stared back.

"Yeah," she continued. "I know you think he's an asshole—and he is—but you know what? You're a bigger asshole. You wouldn't even have any friends if it weren't for Kyle. I know that sounds harsh, but it's true. He's not all bad. His problem is that everybody has been telling him his whole life how great he is, right? But nobody's ever said that to *you*. I mean, I'm just extrapolating here from recent experience, but you know what? You *could* be a great guy. You just need to hear it from the right people. Or maybe you haven't heard it at all. But that's cool. Oh—what's your real name, by the way? Hello?" Liz shrugged and handed the phone back to Kyle. "He hung up."

Kyle shoved the phone in his pocket. "I don't get it. Why?"

"You know why. I want to help you if you help Will."

"I don't believe that," Kyle said. His bad eye began to sting. "Why did you just stick up for me?"

"Because of what you said about Will and me," she said, sitting back down.

Kyle shook his head. "I don't—"

"Because you believe it's true. And I want to believe it's a lie. But I can't." She clasped her hands in front of her and rested them on the place mat, her hair shrouding her face. "Just like I want to believe that I really might write a memoir, or become famous, or whatever. But . . . what you believe. I don't know. I think it might be true."

The words didn't make any sense. They couldn't. If Liz were saying what he thought she was saying . . . but no, she couldn't be. *Could* she? No. He opened his mouth, but before he could ask another question—or hustle her out of this restaurant and back into the car—Will lurched out of the bathroom.

"So, what are you guys whispering about?" he asked jovially, standing over the table. His face was the color of chalk, except for the purple bruises under his eyes.

"Nothing," Liz muttered.

"Liz," Kyle began. "I want you to tell me what the hell—"

"You know what? I'm not hungry after all." She hurried out the door.

Kyle blinked. His throat tightened. For a brief second, he was worried he might start to cry. He looked up at Will.

"Hey, don't sweat it," Will said. "You got nothing to worry about. All siblings fight. That's the nature of the beast." He grinned drunkenly.

"You don't know what's going on here, Will," Kyle mumbled.

"Sure, I do," Will said. "It's a fight between siblings. You and I fight all the time, and we're brothers, and we barely even know each other. See?"

"Always the comedian," Kyle muttered.

"Guilty as charged. Laugh a little! No offense, man, but you got some stuff you have to work out. I don't know what it is, but something's eating at you. I'm speaking from experience. . . . I can tell these things. I mean, look at me. If my uncle hadn't blown himself up, I'd probably be a better driver than *you* by now." He hiccuped. "That's, um, just a theory, of course. I got a C-minus in intro to psych."

Kyle shook his head. But this time, even he had to smile. Not only was Will a complete imbecile, and offensive, and doomed to hell, and *high*—he didn't even make sense anymore. He sounded like a lunatic.

"What in God's name are you talking about, Will?" Kyle demanded.

"To tell you the truth, I have no idea." Will hiccuped again. "I'm just trying to kill some time before the three of us have to get back into that car."

chapter 21

Upon leaving the restaurant, Will discovered that walking was not his strong suit. His feet had turned to Jell-O. He needed to lie down. Something about the drug cocktail he'd consumed in there . . . It wasn't quite working the same way as the one he'd consumed last night. It was making him very tired. Rip Van Winkle tired. But when he pulled the front seat forward so he could slip in back, Liz grabbed his arm.

"I'm going to sit in back," she said. "Will, you're welcome to sit up front until we stop again." She shot Kyle an unreadable psychic-twin look. "I insist."

Will was in no condition to protest. He couldn't even open

his mouth to answer. He slumped down in the front seat and closed his eyes.

* * *

When he awoke with a start, he wasn't sure how much time had passed. A very, very unhealthy blackout-snap-awake pattern was forming. He felt as if he'd been asleep for five minutes, but it must have been a good seven hours or so. The sun was on its way down, hovering just above the horizon to the left of the car. Remarkably, he felt refreshed—not hungover at all, just a little thirsty. (That, and more depressed than he'd ever felt in his life.) But depression was probably healthy. Dr. Brown would likely agree. Will squinted at an approaching sign.

DELAWARE MEMORIAL BRIDGE 13 MILES

His eyes bulged. "Whoa, whoa—wait a second. We're already in *Delaware*?"

Kyle laughed. "What kind of drugs did you take back at Shorty's?" he asked.

"Nothing," Will said uneasily. "I mean, just the rest of the Wellbutrin . . ." Or *was* it Wellbutrin? Mom had a sneaky habit of filling her old prescription bottles—her *legitimate* prescription bottles, that is—with pills she hadn't purchased at the pharmacy. He fished through his jacket pocket for the bottle.

EXP: 9/11/03

Ha! It's all too rich and coincidental, isn't it?

"I finished all the drugs I stole from my mom," he added, tossing the bottle on the floor. Fear prevented him from saying anything more. But it felt good to tell the truth, or at least the truth as far as he knew. Liz had been wise to institute the honesty rule. And believing in lies *was* bad, no matter how sweet they were. No more secrets! He decided to let Kyle do the talking.

"Well, you've been unconscious for nineteen straight hours," Kyle told him in a clinical tone. "You mumbled a lot in your sleep. Oh, and there was one stop to use the bathroom. Do you at least remember the bathroom stop? In Virginia?"

Will forced a smile and nodded, but in reality, he didn't remember it at all—a fact he found utterly terrifying. So . . . the sun wasn't on its way down. It was on its way up. *No more sneaking away for drugs*, he swore to himself. Until now, he'd fooled himself into believing that there was something tragically romantic about treating this trip the way Hunter S. Thompson would have treated it. But Hunter S. Thompson had ended up killing himself too, just like Uncle Pete. And Will didn't want to kill himself. Not quite yet. He glanced back at Liz, who was once again sleeping comfortably in the backseat.

"Liz and I have been taking turns driving, eating, and sleeping," Kyle said, as if Will needed clarification "We've also paid for all food and gas."

Will sank into the smelly upholstery, overcome by powerful waves of shame. Kyle and Liz had subsidized this entire drive, and *he* had spent the paltry remnants of his money on a clandestine drug haul. "Hey, Kyle, I really do appreciate how you guys are trying to help me out here. I mean, I know I haven't been the easiest passenger—"

"Liz and I had to drive up to New York anyway," Kyle cut in.

"Yeah, but . . ." Will smiled.

"What's so funny this time, Mr. Comedian?"

"Just waiting for the punch line. Unless you've done a lot of drugs in the last nineteen hours, I'd say something was up. You're being sort of nice."

Kyle switched lanes. His jaw twitched. "No, I'm not."

"Okay," Will said, swallowing. "I just want to say I'm sorry." He wasn't sure where the apology was coming from—well, he *was*, and it had everything to with Liz—but an internal dam had been punctured, and now he couldn't stop. "I'm sorry for being harsh about your idea to turn the New Democracy into a nationwide thing. Knowing you, you really could pull it off. You already *have* pulled something like that off, with your dating service. Most people don't take initiative like that. It's human nature to let things slide as long as possible without ever having to deal with it—"

"Will?" Kyle interrupted. "Why don't you go back to sleep, okay?"

"I'm sorry. I just wanted to say I was sorry."

"You've said you were sorry about six times now." With one hand on the wheel, Kyle scratched his slicked-back scalp. "Listen: Liz and I were talking while you were passed out. You guys were right. Trying to make a franchise out of it is a lame idea. Anyway, I was being greedy. That's the truth."

Will wanted to say something more, but he couldn't. *Kyle won.* There was no fighting it. Will had taken himself out of the picture with drugs—and in the interim, Kyle had brainwashed his twin. Will didn't give a shit about New Democracy or Kyle's business aspirations. He gave a shit about Liz, and Kyle knew it.

Kyle managed a feeble chuckle. "Liz is a good arguer, you know that?"

Will glanced at Liz again. She hadn't stirred. "Yeah. I guess I do. So you guys made up, huh? What did I tell you? All siblings fight."

"All siblings fight," Kyle echoed.

"Mm-hmm." Will wasn't sure how to wrap this up. *Say something funny*, he ordered himself. *Change the subject. Don't let this devolve into a confession about how I think I might still be in love with my half sister, even though I'm not on drugs anymore.* "So . . . um, speaking of bad ideas, have you come up with a plan to convince Chadwick Wharton that I'm a licensed driver?"

Kyle snorted. "Are you kidding? I'm not that smart. You know, it would help if Dad were here. He was always good at coming up with crazy schemes."

Will turned away and stared out the window at the industrial Delaware wasteland.

Physically, Dad might not be in the car, but spiritually (SPIRITUALLY?), he was omnipresent. His ghost had set the scene with his ridiculous demands; his ghost had put together this ill-fated carpool northward; his ghost had been riding with them the whole way, too—and laughing all along, laughing at their detour, at Will's attempts to drive, at all of Will's inadequacies. . . . Come to think of it, Dad's ghost was probably the only passenger who'd truly enjoyed the trip.

"Why *did* Dad hate me so much?" Will asked. He wasn't talking to Kyle. He wasn't even really talking to anyone, but Kyle answered.

"I don't think Dad hated you. I don't know what his problem was." He paused for a second. "I think it had something to do with your mom."

"Yeah, that's what I think too. But what was it about her that he hated so much? Did she cheat on him or something?"

"How would *I* know?" Kyle asked.

Will's head throbbed. Good question. There was more he wanted to ask Kyle—a *lot* more—but in the end, harping on it would just make Will look like he was fishing for sympathy. Better just to ride out the rest of the drive in silence. They only had a few more hours. And after that, as Will so often reminded himself, they'd never have to see each other again. So he kept his mouth shut. It was the grown-up thing to do.

* * *

Being grown-up was a little more difficult than he would have thought, especially when Liz woke up.

She smiled tentatively at him in the rearview mirror, almost apologetically. But was it an apology for kissing him or an apology for not dealing with it? He smiled back at her, his eyes wandering to her lips . . . and they were dry again, like sandpaper. Detached. Ah, well. He decided not to say anything. He didn't want to piss off Kyle.

After that, the silence became easier.

***

Events came and went, blurring together in the motion of the car. There were opportunities for Will to speak up, but he never did. He kept silent when a cop pulled them over outside of Bordentown, exit 7 on the Jersey Turnpike. He kept silent when the cop demanded to know the significance of the peace sign painted on the car's hood ("Peace!" Liz told him). He even kept silent when the cop stared in disbelief at Will's passport and cackled: "You mean to tell me you're nineteen years old and you don't know how to *drive?*"—and furthermore, when the cop searched the three of them for drugs. (It really *was* a good thing he'd finished off those pills at Shorty's.) He kept silent even though he'd never wanted to brush his teeth so badly in his entire life.

All in all, he kept silent until they were emerging from the fetid darkness of the Lincoln Tunnel into the bright smog of midtown Manhattan. It was 10 a.m. Friday.

This is the end, Will said to himself.

Only then did the Volvo's engine begin to sputter again.

***

"We still haven't come up with a plan!" Liz exclaimed. Her voice was hoarse.

"I know," Kyle said.

"Sounds like this car needs a tune-up," Will remarked.

"How would you know?" Kyle asked.

"I wouldn't. But I have an idea for a plan."

"Oh, yeah? What's that?"

"Well, here goes." Will knew he'd never get Liz alone to talk about what had happened. Kyle would always be there. Just as Dad's ghost would always be there, or Dad's SPIRIT, or whatever . . . and what had happened with Liz would always be there too, haunting Will for the rest of his life. So he would just have to deal with it. He had to accept or banish it. It was up to him to let Dad go, and Pete, and maybe even Liz too. It was up to Will to give up all that wasted energy: the resentment, the despair, the rejection . . . the search for an explanation that would never come. "Kyle, why don't you just drop me off at the Times Square subway station?"

Kyle slowed to a stop at a red light. "You're kidding, right?"

Will shook his head. "Nope."

"Will?" Liz asked from the backseat. "What are you doing?"

"I'm thanking you," he said. He sat up and stretched, his suit jacket peeling off the backseat. He felt calmer than he'd felt in a long while. He knew what to do now: avoid the subject of Liz; focus on the Volvo. "I mean, we all know Dad never wanted me to get the two million in the first place. I bet the money isn't even *there*. Kyle, you sacrificed time, money—your own business—for a half brother you never knew, and you never once asked for anything in return. Well, aside from the Volvo. But that was always for Liz. And Liz . . . what can I say? I don't want to see you again for at least forty years. That's a lie, by the way."

Liz didn't answer.

Kyle made a hissing sound.

"What, Kyle?" Will said.

"You're giving up *now*?" Kyle demanded.

"What do you mean?"

"We're less than ten blocks from Chad's office, and we've come about a thousand miles! No way am I letting this happen. We're all going to meet with Dad's lawyers and open that safe. Will, you are *getting* that money. We've come too far. And the truth is that I want you to have that money, because it's insurance."

Will frowned. "Insurance?"

"Yes, insurance that we won't have to see you ever again. If we get you the money, you'll have gotten what you wanted. And then we can say goodbye. And maybe I do feel a little bad that Dad hated you so much or whatever, but screw it. We're *going* to the office. Even if Chad knows that you don't know how to drive . . . We need to end this thing. I don't want to see you for the next forty years either. . . ." Kyle took a deep breath. "I'll just spell it out for you. Nobody likes a quitter, Will. And that's what you are. A quitter."

Nobody likes a quitter, Will.

The city faded into a dull vacuum. The spinning-wheel universe shrank to the car, encompassing past and present, the living and the dead. In one bold strike, Kyle had succeeded in doing what Will could never do: he'd exorcised Dad's ghost. Kyle had conjured Pete really and truly—and Will *could* see him, without the aid of drugs or drink . . . pretty much stone-cold sober. . . . He could see the mighty Pete sweeping into the stuffy Volvo in his fiery chariot and driving Dad's ghost away, banishing the evil and baptizing them all with the call to action, with the call to split up and embark on an exodus from each other for the rest of their lives.

A tear fell from Will's left eyelash. He hadn't even realized he was crying. He resisted the urge to lean over and hug Kyle or to mention Uncle Pete.

"Will?" Liz whispered. "Are you okay?"

"That's a funny question," he said, his voice strained. "But I want you guys to wait in the car while I go up and talk to Dad's lawyer. I mean it. This is *my* problem."

Kyle didn't respond.

He glanced back at Liz. She said nothing.

* * *

Fifteen minutes later, Kyle pulled up in front of 540 Park Avenue. Will hopped out and stepped inside the luxurious, air-conditioned lobby. He avoided looking at Liz.

A large security guard in a blue uniform sat behind a desk near the door. He regarded Will warily from over the top of a *New York Post*.

"Can I help you?" he asked.

"I'm here to see Chadwick Wharton. My name is Will Shepherd."

"Chadwick Wharton?" the guard repeated. "And your name is . . ."

"Will Shepherd."

The guard picked up the phone and punched in four

numbers. "Will Shetland is here to see you." He nodded and hung up. "Mr. Wharton will be right down."

"Shepherd," Will said. "Will *Shepherd*."

The guard didn't acknowledge the correction. He retreated behind his paper. *Ha!* Will could relate. It was a fitting ending to his journey, this gift of invisibility. He'd been invisible his whole life to Dad, and now the practical joker had won, in spite of the best intentions of Will's half siblings, who were as of now the only people on this planet who actually *knew* him. But Pete had won the true victory. Pete had made Will stand up for himself. Well, Pete and Kyle. And Liz.

Ding!

The elevator doors opened. Dad's lawyer emerged with a full makeover: ponytail, beard trimmed, decked out in a crisp double-breasted gray suit. He flashed Will a perfunctory smile as he strode across the lobby.

When he shook Will's hand, he recoiled. His nose shriveled. "Do you realize that you reek of alcohol?" he asked.

"Sure," Will said. "But you're a drug fiend, right?"

The lawyer sighed. "Shouldn't you be behind the wheel right now?"

"You think I should be behind the wheel in the state I'm in?"

"If you're trying to—"

"I don't know how to drive," Will interrupted. "Story of my life. So if there's nothing else, I just wanted to tell you to forget it. The deal is off. Okay?"

Chadwick Wharton nodded.

He reached into his breast pocket and handed Will an unmarked envelope. "Fine. But this is for you." He flashed Will another inscrutable smile before heading back to the elevator bank. "Goodbye."

"'Bye," Will said.

The elevator doors closed, swallowing Chadwick Wharton.

This is one of those moments, Will realized.

YES. It was one of those moment that required self-control, and dignity, and all the rest of the splendiferous traits that only exist on-screen or in the pages of a novel . . . and Will could *see* it—YES, just like he'd seen Uncle Pete in the car only minutes ago—only this was *real*. He envisioned exactly how a hero (or even an *anti*-hero) would act: he would tear the envelope to shreds with a great shocking noise—*BOOOOOOM!*—and allow the scraps of white paper to flutter to the floor in the morning sunshine . . . and oh, how sweet it would be! And in the midst of this imaginary apocalyptic tempest—while the security guard and Chadwick Wharton stared at him (mortified, of course, unprepared for such a display of strength)—Will would march calmly out of the office and into the new day: unscathed and unafraid, with the sound track blaring and the audience cheering. . . .

And then the vision melted.

Will was alone. The albino security guard bent down and picked up his copy of the *New York Post*. Will tore open the envelope.

* * *

Dear Will,

So I guess if you're reading this, you haven't gotten your license. You're also probably wondering, Why did Dad hate me so much? Well, the truth is, I never hated you. I wanted to hate you. I guess that's why I was such an "enormous shit-bag," as you so eloquently phrased it in your application essay. But I didn't. I couldn't, which is natural, because you're the only child I've ever fathered. You're my only son.

Kyle and Liz aren't mine.

There. I said it.

Incidentally, I've written letters to Kyle and Liz too. I told my attorneys to wait one year after my death to pass the letters on. But you know lawyers, kiddo; you can't trust the bastards. I figure the twins might take the news a little harder than you. That's why I want some time to pass. I don't want to hurt them. Truth is, I'm sick and tired of hurting people, if you can believe it.

Why am I telling you this? Cowardice is part of it. I'm not worried about your seeing them or spending any time with them. Although, who knows? Maybe you'll get along. I always thought you and Liz would dig each other. Anyway, if you *do* see them, will you do your old man a favor? Not that I deserve any favors from you . . . but please keep this revelation to yourself? Cindy and I promised each other that we would never tell anyone, including you. But now that I'm dead, I'm entitled to break the promises made by the living. I guess it's one of the perks that come with the territory.

So, I bet you have some questions. Like, How did this all happen?

Well, not to throw blame around, but it started with your mother. I loved her. That's as best as I can say it. I loved her the way they sing about it in every fucking song under the sun, and I loved her even when she became a wizened, depressing old crone with red nail polish who represents all these loser artists. I could still see the beauty. But the feeling wasn't mutual. . . . More on that in a bit.

The facts: She had an affair with one of her artists right after you were born—a scumbag addict named Ari who OD'd years later. She always loved him, the same way I loved her. Unrequited, unrequited! The point is, I knew we were living a lie. Not that knowing this helped me in any way. Hell, no, son. As soon as I found out she cheated on me, I hit the Rage Highway. I reconnected with some of my brethren, who had all somehow made the collective unspoken decision to switch from psyche-delics to booze and blow. Due to the Jungian uncon-scious? Cindy would say so. . . .

Right. Cindy. She was this chick I knew during the seventies—knew in the biblical sense—and I figured I could hit that action again. (Forgive my crassness.) The problem was, she loved me the way I loved Julia. I didn't know it. How could I know that? How could ANYBODY love me like that? But she confessed: ever since we lost each other, she'd pined after me, and she was convinced that I was THE ONE for her.

I did everything in my power to prove her wrong. I was an asshole to her, not because I didn't like her, but because I still loved Julia so much. I did everything in my power to piss her off: drugs, cynicism . . . the whole deal.

I know that doesn't make any sense. But maybe someday it will.

So, it worked. Cindy grew to loathe me—very fast. And she cheated on me, too. I guess you already figured that part out. But to give Cindy her due, the word *cheating* isn't quite fair in her case. It was a *backslide*. Are you familiar with the concept of the backslide?

It's very Zen, and very alcoholic, and very cold, yet very comforting. It's all about nostalgia. Hooking up with a long-lost screw! In other words, it makes no sense whatsoever in earthly terms, but to a Wiccan or to an enormous shitbag, it does. And I forgive her for it. What else could I do, Will? I did the exact same thing with her. She was *my* backslide: because I was in so much pain over Julia, and because Cindy was so hot, and I was so stoned, it didn't matter that I was shallow and she was humorless. I believed in the lie of the moment. To my credit, the guy she cheated on me with was pretty shallow and humorless too—but he was a hell of a lot better looking than I am, and, as I said, he gave me two amazingly beautiful children. (Not that you aren't beautiful, Will. But you ain't Liz or Kyle.) And I loved them. I truly did and do, even though I was an asshole.

Jesus! Has some of Cindy's shallowness rubbed off on me?

The answer is yes, by the way. You try living for twenty years with a woman who doesn't love you and vice versa! You try pining after a woman who can't and won't love you back! But these are all issues for the After Life, when you and I can hang out in eternity. The reason I separate and capitalize the words is because I don't believe in the "afterlife"—not at least as People of the Book (that's us Jews) see it. I don't see karma or damnation or anything. I see it as a chance to hang. That's all. And that's what we'll do. You and me, Will. I swear it. We're family, man! We'll have a drink and talk about all sorts of shit.

Sorry for the rant or whatever you want to call this letter. Sorry for a lot of things. You know what's weird? You're going to laugh, but all I ever wanted was a family. That's all: a real, loving family, with your mom. By the way, don't worry. I did put some money away for you. Talk to my lawyer about it. On that, you can trust him.

Love,
Dad

PS: I was high as all get out when I wrote this.

PPS: NOT kidding! (Oops, did I write that or just think it? ☺)

* * *

Will looked up. Kyle was suddenly standing beside him.

"What?" Kyle said. "What's it say?"

What's it say? "Uh . . . Where's Liz?" Will croaked. "She should—"

"She went to get coffee," Kyle muttered. "Now look, before you say anything, I've made a decision. And stop looking at me like that . . . because listen: we're entitled to break some rules. So I *am* going to buy this car from you. Like you suggested in Miami. I'm buying it as a gift for Liz. But I'm offering two million dollars. It's non-negotiable."

"Read this first," Will whispered.

Kyle blinked. He looked frightened. Will could understand. He could *definitely* understand, because Will Shepherd was no longer an invisible, no longer a ghost; he was in plain sight, which *was* pretty frightening. Kyle took the letter and skimmed it. His face was a blank mask. He read it a second time, much more carefully. Then he handed it back. He took a moment to breathe.

"The offer is two million," he concluded. "Take it or leave it."

Will felt the floor spinning beneath him. *"What?"*

"There's nothing in that letter that would change my mind," Kyle said. His voice was strong and firm. (Now *there* was self-control!) "You don't get to choose who your family is, Will. You're stuck with them, and you just have to deal with it. I could have done a lot worse. So are you going to take my offer or what?"

Will considered Kyle's offer for a second.

But then he realized there was nothing to consider at all. He already had a counteroffer in mind, and he knew Kyle would definitely accept it. Of course he would. His prick of a brother was a businessman.

"No," Will said. "Here are the new terms. Liz gets to keep the Volvo, on one condition. You guys spend the rest of the summer teaching me how to drive stick. If I don't learn how to drive stick by the time you start college, the Volvo is yours. Deal?"

Kyle hesitated. "We get to choose where we teach you, though. We need a lot of empty space. I'm thinking Jersey."

"Jersey? I hate Jersey."

"It's non-negotiable," Kyle said. He stuck out his hand.

Will shook it. He almost smiled. Almost.

"Deal," they both said.

Liz pushed through the lobby doors and ran toward them. "The coffee in this neighborhood sucks," she said. "I couldn't find anything I liked. Plus, we're illegally parked. We should get going." She glanced between Kyle and Will, then zeroed in on the letter. "What's that?"

"You can't see it," Kyle blurted. He clamped his hand over his mouth. His eyes welled with tears.

"I have to see it," Liz said. She grabbed it from Will's hands. She began to read, slowly at first.

Will studied her eyes as they flashed over the pages. Soon she stopped breathing. Her hands started to shake. The pages rippled, on the verge of breaking apart and exploding in a very noisy and violent fashion.

"Good news, right?" Will choked out once she'd finished.

She looked up, her mouth ajar. And before she could

respond, he lunged for her and hugged her; he hugged her as tightly as he could—a thousand times tighter than when he'd hugged her down south, so tight he could feel her bones through her dress, and she hugged him back and wept a little—and all the while, the letter's revelations exploded in silent bursts through his brain, with just the briefest time delay between the flashes and the impact of what all the lies and truths really meant.

"It *is* good news, Liz," he whispered. "We aren't family after all."

acknowledgments

First, I would like to thank Liesa Abrams, whose initial belief in this book made it possible, and whose heart, talent, and creative genius guided me the entire way. In addition, I would like to thank Eloise Flood, Kristen Pettit, and the rest of the Razorbill crew; you are all rock stars. So are my incredible agents, Jennifer Unter and Edward Necarsulmer IV. You kept the faith! I would also like to thank the members of the writing group where this novel began to take shape: Amy Wilensky, Bowman Hastie, Joanna Hershon, Merrill Feitell, and Gretchen Rubin—I laud you for your invaluable help and insight. (I say, reform the band.) The one who deserves the most credit, as always, is my brilliant and beautiful wife, Jessica, whose love, support, and much-needed criticism never cease to amaze and inspire me. And of course I would like to thank my family (parents, brother, sister, nieces, nephews, aunts, uncle, and in-laws) for their unflagging love and support. Finally, I would like to thank the guitar playing of Tony Iommi, circa 1970–78.